PRIEST

A Novel
By

Morrie Richfield

I would like to dedicate this novel to my friend Baby who passed away with me by her side on September 7, 2013. The world was a better place for the time she was in it.

To Dr. Frances Sutter, thank you for saving my life; I probably wouldn't be here if it were not for you and your team. I'm forever grateful.

I would also like to dedicate this novel to all the dreamers out there and to those of us who see the terrible things we do to each other and think, what if we could all be better?

And to Adge, Kim, Taylor and Jake. I hope the world you will help create will be a better one than we'll leave you.

And to you, Michele, without you I wouldn't be me. All my love always.

The Middle East
1969

By the age of eight August Priest already spoke six different languages and by the time he left high school at nineteen he had mastered just about every language, including all the dialects used in the Arab-Israeli world.

His parents died when he was very young and he had been raised by his aunt and uncle, who were childless by choice—for the most part, August was left to his own devices. His parents had been quite wealthy and had left August a very large inheritance, though it never seemed very important to him.

He grew up watching *Father Knows Best* and *Rin Tin Tin,* television shows that helped him to develop the moral code he lived by. He was also a student of history, especially the history of military warfare. He studied every battle that had ever been written about, and played out scenarios is his mind, focusing on how his versions might have changed the outcome. In the process he became a brilliant military tactician, a man so skilled that the US relied on him to orchestrate every American victory over the next few decades.

When he was still quite young, August began to master a variety of weapons—knives, handguns, rifles—and was such a natural that he easily became an expert. He entered shooting contests all over the country and always won; no one could beat him and in fact no one could even come close: he was like a machine and he never missed a target whether it was moving or stationary.

He was written up in newspapers all over the country and that is what caught the attention of Neil Hawthorne, who had just been made the head a newly formed division at the Central Intelligence Agency. He could see that August was the perfect addition to his new division: he was big and powerful, and he was a master of languages and weapons. Hawthorne was a very ambitious man who wanted status, but who craved power even more. Neil saw that August had a singular quality: he viewed every matter as either right or wrong—for him, there was no middle ground. Hawthorne realized that August Priest was the perfect type to be manipulated, and so in 1968 he recruited him as a CIA operative.

Hawthorne assigned Priest a mission: to seek out potential threats to the United States, which at that time meant threats to the American economy. August was to pose as a college student researching a paper on the Middle East and its people. He was given a contact the agency had been using to get information, and was told that was the best place to start.

In 1969 when he arrived in Jerusalem to start his assignment it didn't take him long to realize that anyone supposedly embedded in groups hostile to America was merely feeding the US whatever it wanted to hear in return for a payment. It didn't even occur to these people that August could understand every word they spoke: they thought he was a young fool and they bragged constantly about how they had so utterly tricked the Americans.

They had no real connection to any groups and the information they offered was of little help to August so he set out to make his own contacts. It didn't take him long to meet a boy named Aziz, who worked in Mahane Yehuda outdoor market in Jerusalem. August guessed he was around sixteen or seventeen, though Aziz would never confirm that, nor would he ever give August his last name. He did want to learn English and August began to teach the boy. Before long Aziz was speaking English so well you would have thought he had been brought up in small town America.

August used his role as a teacher to try to gain Aziz's trust, but trust didn't flow freely in Israel at that time. The 1967 war was still on everyone's minds and August was certain that the Israelis were watching his every move. He had never been very political and, in his mind, he hadn't been sent to the Middle East to decide who was right and who was wrong. He had been sent for one reason: to determine if the conflicts of the region could at some point endanger the American economy. But he could see that that mission was changing very quickly.

It took August a lot longer than he anticipated to get Aziz to trust him enough to start talking freely, but when he open up August was astounded by what he knew. He spoke of the once powerful Ottoman Empire whose defeat in World War I had changed the region forever. The United States and its allies had then redrawn maps, creating new countries, for which they installed their own puppet rulers.

"How do you know all of this, Aziz?" August asked. He was well educated, but he knew nothing of the Ottoman Empire, as it wasn't something that was taught in American schools. He felt as if he was being schooled by this young boy.

"August, that is the problem with you westerners, you see only what is in your best interests," Aziz told him.

"Then tell me what you see, Aziz."

"Look at where we stand, August. This state of Israel—was it here fifty years ago?"

August didn't even try to reply, since he knew Aziz wasn't really asking.

"No, August, it wasn't, and yes, I'm well aware of what the Nazis did to the Jewish people. It was horrible but neither I nor my people had anything to do with that. When the Jewish people needed their own country it was our home they were given."

August wasn't sure that what Aziz said was true, but he could see that it didn't really matter: the point was that it was Aziz's truth. "Tell me more, Aziz," he said.

"Here most of us are born into poverty and despair and that breeds hatred, so, yes, we're angry. August, we can't vote, We've no rights, and our leaders were not chosen by us but by other countries. Look at how your own country was built, August: your ancestors arrived and they either killed the people who lived there, forced them to live by their ways, or exiled them to a place they didn't want to be. Where are your armies now, August? They're in the jungles of Vietnam trying to make those people live by your ways. Someday, August, your armies will come fight here in the Arab world and your people will try to force your way of life on us. Yes, we're angry with America and that anger will grow stronger as long as you keep helping those who keep us in poverty. We're not as ignorant as you Westerners think we're; we realize that without your help and your weapons none of what is happening here would be possible. Today, August, I see you as a possible friend but I fear someday I'll only see you as my enemy."

"Aziz, what do you think life is like in America? There are some Americans who are very wealthy but there are some who live in poverty and in situations much like yours."

Aziz began to laugh. "You want me to believe that in America, the richest country in the world, there are those who live in poverty. August, please don't take me for a fool."

August soon came to realize that Aziz's world view had been carefully shaped and molded. The fact that it was shared by far too many of those his age made him very worried about what the future might bring. Over the next five months he learned a great deal from Aziz and his comrades.

By the time his mission was over and he was ready to leave August understood that these people would never give up their cause. They believed that their home and future had been stolen from them, and that America was to blame.

August had been sent to determine imminent threats to the American economy. What he discovered, though, was that although the threat might not be imminent, it was far more dangerous than anyone could have imagined. These young men grew up hating America; because the US policies toward the Middle East were not going to change, that hatred would continue to grow and at some point would boil over into action.

Aziz came to visit August the night before he left. "August, I have come to think of you as my friend and have learned to trust you, but I think it is time you told me the truth."

August was somewhat taken back by Aziz's words. He thought that his ruse had been very clever and that Aziz had never suspected that August was anything other than what he claimed to be. His superior at the CIA had never said that his mission was covert, he had simply asked him to gather information. That was just what he had done and he saw no harm in telling Aziz the truth. Besides, he had come to think of Aziz as someone who was true to his cause, and he admired him for that.

"The truth, Aziz. Which truth would you like? The truth that I was sent here by my government to determine whether there are potential threats to our sacred economy? The truth that no one in my country has a clue what is really going on here, and if they did I truly doubt they would even care? Or the truth that I too have come to think of you as a friend and that I can see how you have come to hate my country and blame us for your plight? Which truth works best for you, Aziz?"

Aziz smiled walked over to August, put his arms around him, and hugged him. "My friend, perhaps it is time for your people to learn the truth—and who better to tell them than the man they sent to find it?" Aziz spoke as he held August at arms' length, his hands resting on his shoulders.

Suddenly August felt empowered. Maybe he could change what he saw as an injustice. How could his bosses fail to see the danger in allowing the present situation to continue? Surely they would discern the future threat to the US, in the same way he did.

"Yes, Aziz, I promise you this: I'll tell them the truth and I'll do my best to make them understand that your people see us as the demon who controls and oppresses them. I'll tell them that your hatred of us is growing by the day."

"Thank you, August. That is all I can ask of you. Safe journey, my friend," Aziz said as he left the hotel room.

August wasn't sure why he was suddenly feeling like a hero but he was. He was both the early warning system for what might someday be the greatest threat to the US and the man who had the power to change the lives of millions of people who lived under oppressive rule. He wondered if that make him an idealist or just naïve, but at the moment it didn't matter—he knew what he had to do.

He sat down at his typewriter and began to write the report he would turn in when he returned to Washington. He would call it "The Priest Report."

August was certain that he had completed his mission and that he had done an exemplary job. He was thrilled when two days later Neil Hawthorne told him to report to the Pentagon the following day at 11:00 A.M. to discuss his report. August felt certain that he would be congratulated and that his superiors would express their gratitude.

When he arrived at the Pentagon he was escorted into the meeting room by two uniformed officers. To August's surprise the meeting was already in progress and he was told to sit outside the room and wait. One of the officers went into the room while the other waited with August. About ten minutes August was summoned into the room.

The first thing August noticed was that the room was thick with smoke—the cigars reeked. The second thing he noticed was that there were seven people in the room and only seven chairs. There was literally no place for him to sit down. Neil Hawthorne was seated at one end of the table at the other was an officer who didn't even glance at August when he had come in. The remaining five men all wore uniforms reflecting different branches of the military.

"August, do you really believe that these young men are going to end up being one of the greatest threats our county will face in the future?" Hawthorne asked him.

August thought hard before he answered: these men had obviously already come to a conclusion about what he had submitted, and their view differed from his. They thought so little of him and his report that none of them had even bothered to introduce themselves. He could either cover his ass or stay true to his conscience and keep his promise to Aziz. He made the only choice he could live with.

"Yes, sir, I do. I'm not sure anyone realizes the hatred our actions are fostering. Believe me, no people will allow themselves to be dominated forever—eventually they'll rise up. Sir, if history has taught us anything, it is that empires that don't allow their peoples to be free can't last."

One of the men rolled his eyes. "What are they going to do, son—come over here and throw camel shit at us?"

Everyone laughed except August.

"I didn't say that they were planning to attack us, sir, but these people are far from ignorant and they believe that the people who rule over them can only do so either with our help or at the very least, our ambivalence. As I stated in my report, in their minds, we're the great demon."

August knew it was time to stop talking because no one was listening. He knew that if things didn't change men like Aziz would rise up and take revenge against those who had oppressed them—and the US would be at the top of that list. He couldn't understand why these officers couldn't see what was so clear to him.

"Thank you, August, I'll see you back at Langley tomorrow," Hawthorne said as he dismissed August with a wave of his right hand.

What August couldn't know was that on that day Neil Hawthorne was filled with joy; he was full of himself because everything was going exactly as planned, and now he would use August for his own purposes.

After August left the room, the man in the suit at the other end of the table looked up and tapped his pen on the table. The room went quiet. "I want this report buried and I want all records of this meeting buried and I especially want to make sure that that young man is relegated to a position in which he can't cause any trouble. Is that understood?"

The other six men in the room all nodded their heads.

August stood fuming in the hallway; a part of him wanted to walk back in there and rip those men to pieces. He knew at that moment he could have killed each of them and felt no remorse— in fact, he would have enjoyed every moment of it. It was the first time in his adult life he had ever felt that way. He had learned to control his rage when he was still a child. When he was eleven, there had been an incident: he had beaten two older boys so badly that they had spent weeks in the hospital. Even at that age, he realized that he enjoyed hurting others, and that he must use the anger inside him in more productive ways.

He had conquered those feelings and now it was rare for him to feel any normal human emotion. Neil Hawthorne had somehow seen that in him and had planned to use it to his advantage.

That day as August was escorted out of the Pentagon, he knew that the last few months had changed him in ways that would forever alter his life. On the very next day August Priest would be twenty years old.

Chapter 1
Washington, D.C.
2016

"Fuck you, Rells, you bottom-feeding piece of shit!"

The senior aid to the very liberal Democratic Senator from New York yelled those words right before he hung up on his caller, one Jason Rells, whose syndicated column, "Rells Tells," had been dishing out secrets for over fifteen years. This time Rells had been calling to ask if the rumor was true that the married Senator's penis had accidentally ended up in his housekeeper's mouth. Jason knew that it was nothing more than a rumor, which had likely been started by a conservative group. The right wing had been trying to oust the Senator from office for a long time and this was an election year.

But Jason Rells didn't care if it was true—he just liked to rattle people's cages.

At 48, Rells had never been married, though he loved women, and outside of drinking very good single malt scotches, they were his favorite pastime. Women had the same feeling about Jason: he was handsome, well-built, and had an amazing amount of charm when it served his purpose, and that purpose was always to get something from someone, whether it was information or, in the case of a woman he desired, sex, and maybe information, too.

Jason had many acquaintances but no real friends and he preferred it that way. After one of his columns destroyed the political career of an up and coming congressman, Rells told his editor that if he had caught his father cheating on his mother he would have put it on the front page. Jason Rells didn't have a conscience: he didn't believe in second chances and claimed that he didn't regret a single thing he had written. But it didn't start out that way.

Jason Rells started his career as a reporter at a small newspaper in Virginia but he wanted more. He wanted money and he wanted people to know who he was and he didn't care what he had to do it make that happen. He saw how much money the photographers were getting for a candid shot of a celebrity: they were such easy marks even though they spent a fortune trying to avoid being caught off guard. Jason figured that politicians would be an easy mark, too. So he quit his job and moved to suburban Maryland.

It didn't take him long to figure out that the most powerful people were the ones who were most likely to do something incredibly stupid—all that wealth made them think they were untouchable. Jason would do anything to get the dirt. In the beginning he favored disguises— he'd dress up as a homeless person or pretend to be a deaf mute, whatever it took to get close enough to hear something he could use. When he couldn't get close, he used a small parabolic microphone.

He quickly established himself as a force to be reckoned with, a feeling that intoxicated him. He was soon addicted to it.

It was close to lunch time and Jason decided to take walk over to Casey's, a Washington D.C. watering hole. Jason had done very well for himself and his Capitol Hill townhouse was about ten blocks from Casey's. The place had been around for decades and you could pretty much count on finding politicians from both parties and journalists in a temporary truce. Casey's was neutral ground—even Jason Rells respected that and never used anything he saw or heard there.

He knew better: he couldn't risk being barred from the place that had the best sandwiches and burgers in D. C. Besides, he liked the fact that most of the people in there hated his guts.

Snagging a table at lunchtime wasn't easy, but Jason always ate at the bar, where most of the journalist ate. Jason found a seat and as soon as Ralph the bartender saw him he reached for a bottle of single malt.

"Not today, Ralph, just bring me pit beef sandwich and a bottle of water."

"Don't tell me you're on the wagon, Rells," said Billy McMillan, a sportswriter who was sitting on Jason's right. He was called him Big Billy, and he had shared plenty of drinks with Jason over the years. Jason enjoyed talking with Billy: Jason couldn't have cared less about the sports world and Billy thought politics and politicians were beneath him.

"Nah, Billy, just needed a clear head today," Jason answered.

"Since when do you need a clear head to do what you do?" Billy said, laughing.

Jason chuckled. "I'm getting some stuff in today from my requests."

"Shit, are you still doing that Freedom of Information crap?"

"Yup. I know it's a waste of time but I just find it entertaining."

"What the fuck is entertaining about looking at a bunch of pages where most of the words are redacted?" Billy asked him.

Information junkie that he was, Jason sent in requests once a month using different words, hoping someday someone would slip up and he would get something worth writing about. Of course, that had never happened; every document he received had been so redacted you could barely make out a couple sentences. Jason liked to play a game with himself and try to imagine what was really on the pages. "Who knows, Billy, maybe one of these days I'll get lucky," Jason said, smiling.

"You got a better chance of being asked to join those politicians over there for milk and cookies, buddy boy," Billy told him as he got up to leave. He raised his left hand in a half-assed goodbye gesture and didn't even bother to look back.

Jason finished his sandwich, dropped a twenty on the bar, and stood up. "Put it on my tab, Ralph," Jason yelled out as he walked down the bar towards the entrance. He looked around the room and even though Casey's was neutral territory no one bothered to look in his direction as he left.

Now a lot of people would take offense at that, but not Jason Rells: to him, it was a symbol of his power, his position, and his ability to trash their careers, should he decide to make them his next target. Jason headed back to his townhouse eager to see what goodies his requests had returned this time. He had thought up a really wild request and sent it off: he queried the CIA as to whether any priests had ever been suspected of spying for unfriendly governments. That should throw a zinger in the mix.

Chapter 2
The Candidates

2016 was a big year in Washington—it was time to elect a new President. There would also be Senate and congressional seats up for grabs and one thing was certain: as of January 2017 the government would have some new faces, even if the way things worked didn't change all that much.

Like most two-term Presidents, the current one, a Democrat, had started off with great ideas and a new agenda for America. And like most two-term Presidents nearing the end of their term in office, he had ended up with more losses than wins and an approval rating about as high as the temperature on Inauguration Day. In some ways, you can't really blame the President: after all, most Americans don't really know how the system works and they expect the person they elect to really do all the things they said they would—a sure-fire recipe for disappointment.

With both parties' conventions still months away, prospective nominees were looking for an edge, something to set them apart from the rest of the party line rhetoric. And there was one Democrat who had already accomplished that, merely because she was the first woman candidate who had a serious chance of becoming President. Her name was Mallory Hill. She had been a Senator, an Ambassador and the National Security Adviser to the President Garrison in his first term. She was smart, ambitious as they come, but patient, too, and now she knew that her time had finally come. The country was ready for something different and that something was her.

Jim get in here now," Mallory Hill yelled from her office.

Jim Keller had been Mallory's assistant for years: he was hoping that once she was elected she would make him her Chief of Staff.

"What the fuck is this?" she asked, tossing him a copy of a memo she had gotten from her informants in Congress.

Jim already knew what was in the memo: a group of Republican and Democratic Senators and congressmen and their families would be heading to the Middle East next week on a fact- finding mission to assure our friends in the region that we were still strongly supporting them.

"I find it interesting that every name on that list is vying for the nomination of their party. Don't you find that a bit odd?" Mallory asked with a fair amount of sarcasm.

Jim nodded in agreement, knowing her sarcasm would soon turn to something else.

"So why the fuck aren't *we* going to the Middle East, Jim? Did my invitation to this little tour get lost in the mail?" She stood up and yelled for everyone to come into her office.

"All right, people, let me be clear about this! There isn't a chance in hell that I won't be in the Middle East next week—the only difference between me and these idiots is that I going to get there first, so make it happen *now*." She screamed the word *now* at the top of her lungs.

The rest of the staff rushed out of her office, but Jim stayed where he was and waited for her to sit back down at her desk before taking a seat across from her. "So you think this is a slight against the President or just me?" she asked Jim. "Considering that foreign affairs are my specialty and the biggest weakness of the current administration."

"If I know Senator Ramping it's a slight against the President and a slap in your face. I doubt the Senator wants to give you any more opportunities to show how well acquainted you're with the regions' leaders or the problems that exist there," Jim explained.

"But why bring along the families and why invite members of both parties to go together . . . unless—"

"—Unless he wants to show how he is better equipped to deal with these issues than any other potential candidate but one and you're not going to be there," Jim said, interrupting her.

And what better way to show your strength as a leader and your understanding of the importance of keeping their families safe than to bring your own family with you?" Mallory said. "I have to admit, it's a pretty clever move. What are the President's most recent approval numbers on foreign policy?" she asked.

Jim opened the binder he always carried with him. "Only 22% of Americans approve of the way he has handled foreign policy issues."

"Is there any area where his approval rating is lower?"

"No, ma'am."

"Then that's it—we're going to the Middle East. And no press on this until we're about to take off—is that clear?"

"Understood."

Senator Andrew Ramping was the leading Republican contender and most observers thought the nomination was his, unless he made a serious error. True, a serious error could be something as slight as an off camera remark that ended up being on camera—but that wasn't likely to happen to Senator Ramping. He had been in politics his whole life and wasn't the type to make mistakes; in fact, he had never lost an election and had no intention of breaking that streak, especially when it came to the office he had aspired to his whole life.

He was known to be a conservative, though to his most trusted staff and advisor he liked to refer to himself as a Conservomod. He understood the reality of politics: people on the far right thought he was their best hope, but Ramping was a realist—too far to right and you didn't have a prayer of winning the Presidency. Too far to the right and he'd never be able to win the states that mattered, the ones who decide the victor. He knew he had to appeal to the fringes of his party as well as the Tea Party and independents. He had made a point of dropping hints to the effect that he didn't fully support all of Israelis policies, and had even hinted that he might be willing to cut financial and military aid to countries the US had strongly supported in the past. Those positions helped him with the Tea Party and others, but he also made sure to subtly convey that he understood what was necessary to keep Israel safe and secure. In other words, Andrew Rampling was a gifted politician who appeared to always be on the side you wanted him to be on.

Senator Rampling knew that the American people viewed President Garrison as weak and indecisive when it came to foreign policy and national security. So he made sure that everyone knew he was just the opposite, that he was better equipped in those realms than any of his opponents. This was clearly his best strategy—unless his Democratic opponent was so weak that no one would elect her. But Mallory Hill wasn't that opponent: she was as tough as they come and there was little chance he could convince voters to fear her being elected President.

He needed to marginalize her, find ways to keep her out of the spotlight. She already had a strong following—hell, she could make front page news just by changing her hairdo. He was certain that this trip to the Middle East was the way to steal her thunder, and by showing his willingness to bring along the Democrats, especially those vying for the party nomination, he was painting a picture of just how bipartisan a President he would be.

Encouraging people to bring along their families—sure, that would out a human face on the trip, but that that was just another part of his plan. Creating the appearance that Mallory Hill was washed up on the world stage, not nearly as relevant as she pretended to be—now that was the icing on the cake.

Chapter 3
The Discovery

Jason returned to his townhouse eager to see what goodies his latest requests had brought him. At first all he could find were what seemed like fake purchase orders and the usual redacted pages, which he couldn't make any sense of. Then he saw a large manila envelope at the bottom of the box. He pulled it out: time had worn down the ink on the date stamp, but he could make out the year—1969. He undid the metal clasp, thinking how odd it was that the prongs felt almost new, as if no one had touched them in years. Inside the envelope was a binder of the type created by the archaic binding machines popular years ago. He opened the binder and the title page read, "The Priest Report" by August Priest.

He turned the page and realized to his amazement that the document was in its original form—it hadn't been redacted. Jason began to read and quickly muttered to himself, "Oh my fucking god. Those motherfuckers knew what would happen—we were warned decades ago." When he finished reading, he was in shock: this was way more than a story for his column, this was a fucking bombshell that would rock the world. He just kept thinking to himself, *We knew 47 years ago and if we had acted on the information we could have saved hundreds of thousands of lives.*

Jason opened his computer: the first thing he needed to do was verify who August Priest was and find out if he was still alive. Jason did a search and came up with nothing: not a single hit on the name August Priest. He even tried "August" as the guy's middle name, but still nothing. He wasn't even sure which agency has sent him the report, and then it dawned on him. It was the request he had sent to the CIA inquiring about whether any priests had been suspected of spying. Shit, one of his stupidest requests had paid off.

He got on the phone with the CIA and after about 45 minutes he was able to verify that August Priest had been an employee from 1968 until 2005, but that was all the information they had on him. He was even able to get the very nice young lady to tell him that they had no current address on Priest, nor did they know whether he was alive. Jason wished they had given him more but the fact that they had verified his employment would be enough to get the *Post* to print what would be front page news.

Jason made it over the paper in record time and was sitting in the editor's office watching his face as he read the report.

"Oh my god, do you know what you have here?" Larry Molson asked.

Larry was an old-time newspaperman and believed that good reporters found stories, not the other way around.

"Yes, Larry I do, and I checked and verified that Priest worked at the CIA from '68 to 2005 but there is no record of this guy anywhere."

"Jason, this is an indictment on every administration in the last forty seven years," Larry told him.

Larry picked up the phone and asked for his assistant to come in. She opened the door and stuck her head in the office. "Shelly, I need you to call over to the CIA right now and verify that a man name August Priest was in their employ from 1968 to 2005, and if he was, get me everything you can find about this guy right now." He turned to Jason. "Sorry, but this is way too big a story to not double a triple check everything about it."

"I understand," Jason replied. "Maybe you'll have more luck than I did. I'd love to find this guy alive and talk to him."

About ten minutes later Shelly walked into Larry office and put a single piece of paper on his desk, and stood there waiting for him to read it.

"Okay he did work for them from '68 to 2005, but is this all you could find on this guy?" Larry asked as he handed the paper to Jason.

Jason read the details, although it wasn't much: Priest had been married, but his wife had died. His whereabouts were unknown. He also had a daughter, Emily, but if she was using the last name of Priest she wasn't in any database anywhere. Her whereabouts were unknown.

"What about his pension? He worked for the government for over thirty-five years—he must be getting checks sent somewhere," Jason said.

"Nope, tried that too," Shelly replied. "He turned down his pension no checks and no trace of Mr. August Priest."

Larry handed the report to back to Jason. "I want you to make copies of this and then I want you to put the original someplace where it will not be found. And then you run this on page one. Hell of fucking job Jason," Larry said as he reached out to shake Jason's hand.

Shelly caught up to Jason after he left Larry's office. She grabbed him by the arm and he turned around to face her. "Jason, you be really careful with this," she told him.

"Why, Shelly?' Jason could see she was worried.

"This guy has no social security number, no birth record, and no tax returns— even the IRS records on him are gone. Do you have idea how much pull it would take to do all that?" she said.

"Thanks, Shelly. I appreciate you giving me the warning but what that tells me is that someone went out of their way to keep this guy from being found. So this report must be just a small part of the picture and I want to see the whole fucking thing," Jason answered.

"All right, macho man, but watch your ass 'cause you better believe once this runs a whole lot of people are going to be looking for it," Shelly said, walking away from him.

Jason had been threatened before—sometimes once or twice a day, for that matter. But it was mostly just some idiot who had much bigger problems than Jason and he had never even had someone take a punch at him in all the years he'd been writing his column.

He wondered, though, did Shelly have a point? Was this different? In Jason's mind, he was dealing with a 47-year-old report written by someone who maybe wasn't even alive. But he'd probably find out after tomorrow because in the next 24 hours the whole world was going to know the name August Priest and he figured that if the guy was alive front-page news would bring him out of hiding. If not, maybe someone else with knowledge about August Priest would come forward. Jason thought there had to be more than just a report. What had Priest's real mission been back in 1969?

Chapter 4
The White House

The next day the front page headline of *The Washington Post* read, "We knew. We were warned, and we didn't do anything."

The Priest Report was published it is entirety along with a brief "Rells Tells" column that explained what little was known about August Priest and described how Jason Rells had found the report.

President Martin Garrison called a meeting at noon in the oval office. The Directors of the C.I.A. and the FBI were ordered to attend, as well as his National Security adviser, the head the joint chiefs, and his White House chief of staff. Garrison made it very clear to these men that he expected answers.

When the four men entered the oval office the President was still sitting behind his desk, not in the center of the room, his usual spot, where he liked to sit to make the surroundings more cordial. He was reading the story in the *Washington Post* and didn't even bother to look up as the men entered the room. He was obviously not in the mood to be cordial.

He looked up at the men after they were seated and turned his attention to Kent Baggart, the current director of the Central Intelligence Agency. "Kent, can you explain to me what the hell this is? Who is this guy and how could something like this have existed for forty-seven years without anyone bothering to fucking read it?" the President asked, raising his voice. "I want this man found and I want him brought to this office as soon as possible," he added, pointing a finger at each person in the room. "Do any of you have a clue how this is going to look to the American people? Hell, how is this going to look to the world?"

"Mr. President, this is what I have managed to piece together," Kent Baggart told him. "August Priest was recruited by Neil Hawthorne, the former director of the CIA."

"That Neil Hawthorne" the President said.

"Yes, sir, but back in those days Hawthorne was working his way up the ladder and he saw the Middle East as a hotbed of the future. For some reason, which is still unclear, he sent Priest to Israel."

"So Hawthorne sends the kid to the region—why he does this, we still have no idea. No idea why he was there or what his original mission was. What we do know is that when Priest returned there was a meeting at the Pentagon, and at least six people were in that room, including someone pretty high up from the White House. The person—and once again, we don't know who ordered the report—buried the damn thing. Obviously, it not deep enough. Priest spent the remainder of his career as an analyst, never seeing anything that sensitive in nature. We believe that Hawthorne used his knowledge of the report and the meeting to rise up in the Agency and even to become Director, although we weren't 100% sure about any of this," Baggart added.

"What happened to August Priest—where is he?" the President asked.

"Well, that is the tricky part—we don't know," Baggart answered.

"What do mean—you don't know," the President replied angrily.

"This may not be 100% accurate but what we believe that when August Priest left the Agency in 2005 Hawthorne made some kind of deal with him and his records were wiped clean. We can't find any trace of his tax returns, his social security number doesn't come up, and there are no utility bills or bills of any kind in his name."

The President was becoming visibly angry. "What about his government pension—those checks must be going somewhere."

"That's another problem, Mr. President. He is not receiving any pension checks. Sir, we've got no more proof that he is alive than we do that he's dead," Baggart said.

"All right, can anyone tell me anything that doesn't begin with 'we believe,' or 'we aren't 100% sure'?" the President asked, looking around at each of the men. He paused for a moment awaiting an answer, but no one replied before he continued. "So we have a dead former CIA director who sent someone on an unknown mission in 1969. This person comes back and writes a report which says that we'll be attacked—and I quote, 'with whatever they might be able to use as a weapon,' at some future date unless our government changes its policies in the region. This same CIA director somehow used this report to his advantage and used his position to make this August Priest disappear. It's possible that Priest is dead, but then chances are everyone who was in that meeting forty- seven years ago is dead. The report is mistakenly sent in its entirety to Jason Rells, who is without a doubt the most unconscionable journalist in D.C., and it ends up on the front page of the *Washington Post*. And now it is going to be used to show that we did exactly what we were told *not* to do and that we were aware that the consequences of those actions would likely provoke future attacks on American interests and citizens. Does that about cover it, gentlemen?" The President looked around the room before taking a seat.

Nobody said a word for a good two minutes and then FBI director Frank Linden began to speak. "Mr. President, I have ordered a full investigation into August Priest and my people are at former director Hawthorne's home as I speak conducting a search for any leads on what really happened in 1969. If August Priest is still alive, we'll find him and we'll bring him in, sir."

"Frank, let me make myself very clear. Should you find Mr. Priest, I want to be informed before you take any action. As far as anyone in this room is concerned, this man is not a criminal and is not wanted for any crime. He is not to be taken into custody. Do you understand?"

"Yes, sir," Frank Linden replied. "All right, we're done—except you, Rob. Get me some answers fast and keep an eye on Rells. If anyone can find August Priest, that S.O.B can."

Robert Nathans had been the President White House chief of staff since the beginning and he was also a trusted friend. Robert walked the other men to the door and then turned back towards the President, who was now sitting on the couch in the center of the room.

"How bad is the kickback on this going to be?" the President asked.

"Well, sir, I'm afraid it is going to be a field day for our opposition; it's not going to matter to anyone that forty-seven years ago it was a Republican in your chair. They're just going to see that that the government knew and didn't do anything, and our biggest problem is that we know almost nothing about what really happened back then."

"Do you think there is a chance that this Priest fellow might still be alive, Rob?"

"After all this time I'm doubtful, sir, which means at some point we're going to have make some sort of statement."

"What do you suggest, Rob?"

"Well, sir, first I think we need to issue a statement that says we, unlike the administration in 1969, are fully committed to protecting our people from any power, foreign or domestic, and that we're launching a full investigation of the events that led to the conclusions in this report."

"Do you really think that will calm things down?" the President asked.

"No, sir, this is a shit storm but at least it gives us a little time to try to get some facts. At some point, we'll have to tell the American people and our allies something and right now we're pretty clueless."

"What about Rells, Rob, do you think he knows anything else about this?"

"That man is dangerous—with or without the facts, he may be your worst nightmare. I'll see what I can find out, sir. Should I issue the statement?"

"Yes, do it right away and keep me informed," the President told him as he got up to leave the Oval Office.

Chapter 5
Discovery

Jason Rells was feeling pretty damn full of himself. His name had been mentioned everywhere: the report was being talked about on every television and radio station, and he had become a social media hero in just a few hours. The most fun was listening to the conspiracy theory zealots as they came up with reasons as to why this information had been held back for so many years.

When the White House issued a statement, Jason knew what he had to do. He walked into Larry Molson's office and shut the door. "They don't know shit," Jason said.

Larry just stared at him as he waited for what was coming next.

"He's alive, Larry. I know it."

"What makes you so sure, Jason?"

"Would you need to go to all the trouble of hiding someone if they were dead?"

Larry looked at him and smiled. Jason did have a point and Larry knew that if Priest could be found and he agreed to an interview, it would be Pulitzer time for Rells, no doubt. "Let's say you're right. How do you plan on finding him? I'll bet half the government is also looking for him."

"I haven't gotten that far yet but there must be some clue somewhere; no one just disappears without a trace and I don't think this man wanted to disappear."

"What makes you think that, Jason?"

"Larry, do you think anyone would have thought there was even an ounce of validity to this report back in sixty-nine? This guy must have been laughed out of the room and he probably knew that but he wrote it anyway. A man like that doesn't hide, not unless he has no choice."

Larry picked up his phone and called Shelly into the room. "Shelly, Jason believes August Priest is still alive, and for some crazy reason, I think he might be right, so give him anything he needs."

Shelly nodded. "Whatever you say, boss." Shelly Andrews had been Larry Molson's assistant for fourteen years and she had been there while many important stories unfolded and many important people had been taken down, but she had never had the feeling she had now. She couldn't put her finger on it but something about this August Priest character made her uncomfortable.

Once Jason had left Larry's office and had gone back to his desk, Shelly approached him and asked sarcastically, "So what do you need to help you find your mystery man?"

Jason looked up at her. Shelly was more than just Larry's assistant; she kept the place running smoothly and Jason had learned a long time ago that she had damn good instincts about where a story should go. Jason often wondered why she had never become a reporter. One of these days he'd have to ask her about that.

Jason suspected that Shelly didn't want him to pursue the issue any further, but he wasn't sure why. "What is it about this guy that has you spooked?" he asked. "I know you want me and the paper to drop it."

"I can't put my finger on it but it just doesn't feel right. We have no idea who this man is, no idea what his job at the agency was, and you're basing your conclusions on a report he wrote forty-seven years ago. Has it occurred to you that this man's identity was purposely wiped out and maybe he doesn't want to be found? I agree that there is more to this than just that report but unlike you I think it might be better left unknown."

"I hear you, Shelly, but something tells me I need to keep going on this—I need to find this guy," Jason told her.

"That's your ego talking, Jason. Just remember this: some stories shouldn't be told and I just hope that if this turns out to be one of them you won't let that ego of yours get in the way of your common sense. Let me know when you figure out what you need," Shelly said as she turned to walk back to her desk.

The next day Jason didn't have any answers and he was no closer to finding August Priest. The story was gaining traction and he was seeing headlines in other papers across the country, all asking the same question: "Who is August Priest?" He was getting calls to come on talk shows, both radio and television. Normally he would jump at the chance for attention but he knew that he had nothing to say other than what was already out there, and he didn't want anyone to know he was as much in the dark as they were.

His voicemail was full so no one could even leave him a message, and that was a good thing: he didn't want to be reminded that he was getting nowhere and had nothing more to report. Shelly came over to his desk and this time she had a piece of paper in her hand. "You know your voicemail is full," she told him.

"Yeah, I know. Haven't had time to check it."

"Yeah, I can see how incredibly busy you're," she said, this time her sarcasm was full bore. She handed him the paper.

"What's this?" he asked.

"This woman has been trying to reach you, and when she couldn't she asked for the editor, so I spoke to her. I think you should call her. She seemed like she really needs to speak with you."

Jason gave her one of those what-the-fuck looks and she gave it right back to him.

"Do it for me, okay?" she said as she dropped the paper on his desk.

Jason stared at the slip of paper; the only thing on it was a phone number with a Maryland area code. He didn't think it was worth his time to make the call, but it would be worse to be on Shelly's shit list. He dialed the number and a woman's voice said hello.

"My name is Jason Rells and I understand you've been trying to contact me."

"Thank you for returning my call, Mr. Rells. My name is Emily Hamilton and I was wondering if we could meet. I have something I'd to speak with you about."

Jason was certain he was wasting his time and almost hung up on her.

"Ms. Hamilton, I'm quite busy at the moment."

She didn't reply and hoped she had hung up.

"Mr. Rells, I was born Emily Priest, August Priest is my father. I wonder if your schedule might open up now?"

Jason thought for a moment before answering; his work had taught him not to be too trusting of people. "Ms. Hamilton, I'm sure you will understand if ask you for some proof that what you just told me is the truth," he replied.

"I had a feeling you would be skeptical, Mr. Rells. Give me your cell phone number and I'll send you the proof you need. Once you verify that I'm who I say, then call me back."

Jason gave her his cell and in the next few minutes texts began coming in: everything from her birth certificate to photos of her with her parents. Jason walked over to Shelly's desk and handed her his phone. "The woman you wanted me to call back—can you check out these texts and find out if she's for real?"

Shelly looked at the text messages and then back up at Jason. "Damn. Give me a few minutes and don't stand over me."

Jason knocked on Larry Molson's door and though Larry was on the phone he motioned for Jason to come in. When Larry finished his call Jason told him what had just happened and by the time he had finished Shelly walked into the office.

"Well?" Larry said to her.

"Dr. Emily Hamilton was indeed born Emily Priest, her father was August Priest, her mother was Margaret Hamilton Priest. Dr. Hamilton is a cardiothoracic surgeon at Johns Hopkins and she is considered one of the best in her field. She is telling the truth and now we have a face to put with the man."

"Well, the face we have is not going to be what he looks like now but at least we know he is out there somewhere," Jason told them.

"What makes you think that" Shelly asked.

"Because of what his daughter said: she told me, 'August Priest *is* my father,' not 'August Priest *was* my father.' I told you he was alive."

Larry Molson was thrilled: the story was getting some legs. "Well, Jason, go back to her and be charming—she is the only lead we have."

Jason went back to his desk and dialed the number once again, and the same female voice said hello.

"Hello. I'm not sure if I should address you as Dr. Hamilton or Dr. Priest," Jason said.

"Call me Emily, Mr. Rells, and I assume since we're chatting because you've been able to verify my identity."

"Yes, Emily, we have, and please call me Jason."

"All right, Jason, I do have one condition before I agree to meet with you."

Shit, Jason thought to himself, *she* called *me* and she never said anything about having a fucking condition. Then he realized: she had known better than to bring up a condition before he could verify her identity. He smiled to himself, knowing that he was going to agree to her condition. Well played, he thought, and made a mental note of that for when they met.

"What is your condition, Emily?" he asked.

"This will not be an interview, Mr. Rells. It will merely be a conversation between two people and I'll bring a document I'll ask you to sign saying that you agree to my condition and that I'm not agreeing to an interview. You may take notes but no recording devices—do you agree to my conditions, Jason?"

"Yes," Jason answered.

"Thank you. I did a bit of research on you as well and what I found leads me to believe that we live by different moral codes. I don't want my name in any gossip column. I'm sure you can understand that in my line of work distractions can have terrible consequences."

"I understand, Emily. Where can we meet?"

"There is a coffee shop called Maggie's right across from the hospital. I'll meet you there in two hours."

"Agreed, how will I recognize you?"

"I doubt there will be very many six foot tall women in scrubs with short blonde hair in there, but don't worry, I know what you look like."

Jason Rells wasn't used to having conditions put on him, but this time he knew he had little choice but to accept them. After all, she wasn't the story—her father was—and through her he would find him. Jason filled Larry in before he left; at first, Larry wasn't happy about the conditions but he quickly came to see that Jason had made the right call.

Jason decided to get to Maggie's early and be there when Emily arrived. He found the place easily, grabbed an empty table and decided to order something to eat while he waited. He was somewhat surprised when he looked at the menu; apparently, Maggie's was well known and had been featured on many television shows. Everything was made in house and the previous year they had received an award for best chicken salad sandwich in the country. Damn, Jason thought, they actually give awards to chicken salad sandwiches.

He ordered the award-winning sandwich and after the first bite he was a believer: It was the best sandwich he had ever had. He finished it, gave the waitress his compliments, and waited for Emily to arrive. For the first time in a long time he felt truly excited about his work. Digging up dirt on politicians was financially rewarding but it wasn't real journalism and though he might on occasion uncover some misappropriated reelection campaign funds, his discoveries were far from earth shattering.

There was no way to measure the lives that had been lost over the past forty-seven years, lives that could have been saved if this report hadn't been ignored and stuffed into a box somewhere. Of course, this was Jason's version of what had happened back then; he hoped August Priest would turn out to be the hero in all of this and would be the man Jason had imagined he was.

Jason's thoughts were interrupted when a tall blonde who walked in. He stood up as she walked towards him. Even through scrubs didn't flatter anyone, Jason could tell she had an athletic build. Her hair was short and she wore very little makeup. He noted that if she had wanted to be, she would have been very attractive, but it appeared she did everything she could to underplay her looks. She also seemed to have underplayed her height: she wore flats and was easily 6' 2" or even a bit taller. She walked over to the table and extended her right hand, and they shook.

"Very nice to meet you, Emily, please sit down."

As soon as she was seated, she took a piece of paper out of her pocket, unfolded it, and placed it on the table in front of Jason. "As agreed, Mr. Rells," she said, handing him a pen.

Jason looked over the paper: it was exactly what she had said it would be, and he signed it.

"Please hold this page at eye level," she requested as she aimed her cell phone and took a picture of him holding the signed document.

"I thought you said no photos," Jason said.

"I said no photos on your end. I never said anything about me," she answered with a smile.

"You're not at all what I expected, Emily, but I think you've probably heard that many times before."

Emily smiled slightly to indicate the end of the pleasantries.

"Did you know that your father had written this report?" Jason asked.

"I don't want to disappoint you, Mr. Rells, but the last time I saw or heard from my father was the day of my mother's funeral."

"When was that?"

"That was 1995—over twenty years ago."

Jason was a bit taken aback; he wondered if this meeting was a waste of time—after all, what could she possibly tell him? "When you said, 'August Priest is my father,' I felt you were indicating that he is alive. Did you misspeak?"

"No, Mr. Rells, my father is alive and that is why I asked you to meet me."

"I don't understand. How do you know, and why me?"

"My father's parents were very wealthy and though they died when he was very young that trust fund was never touched. My father had little use for money and that fund is to pass to me upon his death. The documents verifying that were sent to me years ago, so if he were dead, I would now be a very wealthy woman."

"So this is about money?"

Emily's face tightened up and Jason could see in her expression that he had just said the wrong thing.

"Money, Mr. Rells. I couldn't care less about the money, and just for your information, if I ever do get the money it will go charity. You're here because I know you won't stop 'til you find my father. And I want you to bring him a message from me." She handed him a sealed envelope. "I trust you will not open this; it has nothing to do with your story, and is merely a daughter's plea to see her father once again. I have no other family, Mr. Rells, he is all I have."

"I'm sorry I offended you, Emily. I'll deliver this for you but I'm going to need to know anything that might help me find him, because someone did a remarkable job of making him disappear."

"Do you know what he did at the CIA? I didn't know my father very well when I was growing up. I was sent to boarding school at a very early age, but before I was sent away my mother made sure to send her journal along with me. That journal was about my father and the man that she had once called the kindest and most caring person she had ever met, a man who became someone very different as the years went by. In the journal, she wrote that he never hurt her and that although she knew he loved her and me, he was haunted by something that he would never discuss, something that ate away at him until there was nothing left of the man she had married.

There was some mention about what he did; I don't think my mother ever truly believed him when he told her that all he did was handle files. She did make mention of the fact he had go away at times and she didn't think someone who only handled files would need to travel."

"Is that all you know about him, Emily?"

"I'm not a fool, Mr. Rells. I know that you're not going to be the only one looking for him. After I read that report I realized that, whatever my father was, he was no file clerk. I know he loved my mother and me, and if he has stayed hidden from us this long, I have no doubt there is a good reason for it. You may want him so you can exploit him, but you need him alive for that, but I'm not so certain that whoever else may want to find him cares whether he is alive. I'm going to give you some papers that might help you find him," she said, handing Jason another envelope. "You will find copies of deeds to parcels of land that have been in our family for generations. I believe these might lead you to him."

"Thank you, Emily, but why are you trusting me with this?"

"Don't take this the wrong way, Mr. Rells, but you're a narcissistic egomaniac and I'm convinced that you won't share your glory or information with anyone. Why? Because you want to be the one to interview the man who wrote that report and you want to shove that right in the face of our government. Have I missed anything?"

Jason was taken back. Most people would have been insulted by the words that had come out of Emily's mouth but Jason was more concerned that he was that transparent. He was, after all, everything she had described him to be and he was ashamed of that. In his mind, to do his job, there was no way else he could be. "No, Emily, I think you're right on the money; thank you for meeting with me. When I find him I'll make sure he gets your envelope, still sealed." Emily stood up as Jason did and he reached out to shake her hand. "It was very nice to have met you, Emily."

"Thank you for taking the time today. And Mr. Rells, be careful: my mother said that my father had a dark side he never let her see. She wrote in her journal that if it ever came out, she would never want to be around." She shook Jason's hand and then walked out of Maggie's.

Somehow he knew they would meet again.

Chapter 6
Blowback

As expected, the Priest Report had been reprinted in almost every newspaper in the world. There were protests against the United States in all the usual places. Even domestically there were sit-ins and silent vigils and everyone from our allies to our enemies wanted the same thing: answers. Answers President Martin Garrison didn't have, so once again Kent Baggart, Frank Linden, and Robert Nathans were in the oval office with the President.

"All right, let's hear it—what have you found out?" the President asked, directing his question to the two directors sitting in front of him.

"We searched Hawthorne's house and we found a lot more than we could have imagined, Mr. President," FBI Director Linden answered.

"What did you find? I want to know everything," the President told him a very authoritative voice.

"Well, sir, we did find a copy of the report that the *Post* published along with Hawthorne's notes from the meeting at the Pentagon. We also found the names of all those in attendance and, as suspected, they're all dead."

"What about Priest? Where is he, and what has Rells been up to?" the President asked.

"We've been unable to determine whether Mr. Priest is alive, and so far, Jason Rells hasn't written another word and he has turned down numerous requests for interviews, so we've concluded that, other than the copy of the report that was printed, he has no further knowledge of Mr. Priest," Frank Linden answered.

He failed to mention to the President, however, that he had ignored the order to follow Jason Rells. He didn't think some gossip columnist could find someone faster than his agency could, and it was an insult to him to even suggest such a thing.

"So this is all you managed to get?" the President asked.

"Not exactly, sir, we found a great deal more and I'm afraid some of it we're still going through," Linden answered.

"Explain."

"Mr. President, while Neil Hawthorne was running the CIA he was also running his own network using outside contractors and an assassin that most of us used to think was a myth but as it turns out he was Hawthorne's weapon of choice and we believe that all the men who were in that meeting at the Pentagon met their death at the hands of this assassin," Linden told him.

"Go on, Mr. Linden, this is just getting better by the moment," the President told him. Everyone in the room could see that this news didn't please him.

"We also found encrypted files that we turned over to the CIA in hopes that their people can break the encryption. But it's not like anything we've come across before," Linden told him.

The President looked at CIA Director Kent Baggart. "When will you crack the encryption? I want to know what's on those files."

"I have my best team on it, sir, but it might take a few days," Baggart replied.

"What about this mythical assassin—could he be the reason Priest disappeared?" the President asked.

"Sir, there was a rumor in the agency for years about this assassin who everyone called The Ghost. No one ever believed he was for real but any time someone the agency wanted out of the picture suddenly died, the word would spread that The Ghost had got him," Baggart said.

"So it seems that we now have even more questions than we did before. Rob, do you have anything to add?" the President asked, looking over at his chief of staff.

"I think that those encrypted files are going to give some idea of exactly what Hawthorne was up to but I have a couple questions. First, you said all the men in the meeting are now dead—were their deaths in any way suspicious? Then there's Rells: he doesn't seem like the type to drop something like this, so why aren't we hearing any more from him on this? As far as I'm aware, he has contacted no one for an on the record comment about the report. I'm sorry but I'm just not buying the idea that he has nothing else," Rob Nathans said.

"Do we know how those men died?" the President asked, echoing his chief of staff.

"No, sir, we weren't looking into that side of things, we were only trying to determine if anyone knew anything the report," Frank Linden answered.

"Thank you, Frank. Kent, now please go and find me some real answers," the President said.

The two men nodded, and then got up and left the President's office.

The President looked over at Rob Nathans and shook his head. "You know, Rob, it's one thing to have to clean up your own shit, but it's quite another when you're forced to clean up someone else's shit," the President told him.

"What are you thinking, Mr. President?"

"What I'm thinking, Rob, is the further we go down this rabbit hole, the more that things I'd rather not share with anyone are coming up. What kind of a game was Hawthorne playing and why didn't any of this come out earlier? I'm worried about what's in those files and I'm worried about what Rells knows. I agree with you—that bastard isn't going to let this go. He knows something more than what he printed. My guess is, he just can't prove it yet," the President told him.

"Let's put this in worst-case scenario, sir. If it turns out that Hawthorne was running his own off-the-books operations and he controlled this Ghost to do his dirty work and Priest is in hiding because he fears for his life. We can spin all that to make it work for us, sir, put it all out there for everyone to see. You didn't appoint Hawthorne—he wasn't director when you took office and this report was written when you were two years old. Whatever Rells knows can't hurt you; in fact, letting him bring the story to light might help. We just comment on the errors of past administrations. I see no downside to any of this, sir, at least, from your standpoint."

"Are you suggesting that we give Rells information, Rob?"

"No sir. What I'm suggesting is that we don't get in his way and if he needs to be pointed in the right direction we may be able to show him the way."

"For now, just leave him be and don't point anything anywhere without checking with me first. Are we clear on that?"

"Yes, Mr. President."

"What else have you got?" the President asked.

"I heard from Jim Keller. Mallory is going to Tel Aviv tomorrow—she intends to get there before Senator Rampling and the rest of the Republican tour group arrive."

Martin Garrison knew Mallory Hill very well. He knew that she could have been sitting in his chair if the party leaders hadn't decided that he was the better choice at the time. He also knew that she had to go on what he knew and well as she did was a waste of time. There was no reason for any of them to be going because the whole thing was a political circus and the Israelis knew it too, but out of courtesy they would comply.

"Rampling is an asshole, Rob, and he always has been, but he loves the camera and will do anything for five minutes in primetime."

"The Senator is a bit of a prima donna, sir, but he'll likely get the nod and be the Republican nominee. Since the report was published, his little tour group is now up to eighteen legislators and their families. With support staff, we're guessing a little over a hundred people will be going."

The President shook his head and let out a slight chuckle. "I understand why Rampling is doing this and a few of the others, but why are eighteen Senators and Congressmen taking their families into an area that no one can ever guarantee is entirely safe?"

"We believe there are two reasons: the first and the original reason is that your last poll numbers on foreign policy were pretty weak and Republicans want to show voters they're more adept than you are, and then there's the report."

"What does the report have to do with any of this?" the President said, interrupting the explanation.

"Sir, I know you don't listen to the talking heads but some of them have spun that report and being anti-Israeli and it is likely the remainder of the group signed on to appease the Jewish vote."

"That report is forty-seven years old, but you know what I think, Rob."

"You've never commented on the report, sir, and I assumed you didn't feel the need to."

The President looked Rob straight in the eye. "Just between the two of us, Rob, that report may have been written forty-seven years ago but what it says is just as true now as it was back then. We fucked up back then and we've been fucking up ever since; I can't even guess at how much blood this country has on its hands simply because a group of men decided forty-seven years ago to ignore what that man Priest predicted. You could say he was a visionary, but I don't believe that for second. He just told the truth and that is a rarity, especially when we speak of the Middle East. You see, Rob, instead of using our influence and power, we always have our heads so far up someone's ass that we can't see a damn thing. Mr. Priest didn't have to worry about that and if anyone had the guts to tell it like it is, they'd be saying exactly what he did forty-seven years ago. There's nothing in that report that is anti-Israeli, and the Israelis know that as well. The problem We've today, Rob, is that we're so busy trying to appease one group and piss off some other group that we lose sight of what's the right thing to do. I hope they find Priest because I'd like to shake his hand and thank him."

It had been a long time since Rob had heard Martin Garrison speak that way and he was glad to see that he was acting like his old self once again. After almost eight years in the White House

Garrison was no longer the man he once was. He had been a champion of social change and had campaigned on balancing the scales between the rich and the poor, claiming he would do his best to help those in need. Too bad reality had slapped him in the face early in his first term and the opposition fought him every step of the way. They were determined to never give him a win on anything, no matter what the cost to the country. Rob understood that the problem with the modern political system: most Americans had no clue about how it really worked. They elected someone President because they liked what he or maybe she stood for, but then they elected a bunch more people who believed the exact opposite.

Then a couple years would go by and the President couldn't do what he promised because of those people that we fellow Americans also elected, and we blamed the President because, after all, he is the President and he should be able to do what he said. Rob chalked it up to the state of modern American politics: that was why nothing had gotten done and nothing of true importance would likely be done anytime soon.

That was how Rob Nathan's saw things and for that reason when the President left office he would leave as well. He had spent all his adult life in politics but he no longer saw it as a way to serve his country; the people controlling politics now had only their self-interests in mind.

Rob wasn't sure what to make of August Priest—so little was known about him. Was he the hero the President seemed to want him to be or was he just an idealistic dreamer? Rob did agree with one thing the President had said: it must have taken guts to write and present that report. In those days no one would have ever imagined an attack on American soil was possible.

Chapter 7
Lives Lost

Jason Rells was driving to his home instead of going back to the newspaper. Emily was right: he didn't want anyone to know what he was doing and at the moment he didn't want to bring Larry in, at least not until he had a chance to determine if the information Emily had given him would be of any help.

Jason took out the envelope and examined its contents. There were copies of deeds and land records for hundreds of acres, some going back to the late 1800s. Emily had done some of his work for him: she had gone searching herself and she must have been at it awhile since the dates of some of the correspondence went back over two years. Jason smiled to himself, thinking, very clever, Emily, let me do the rest of the work for you.

The properties had exchanged owners numerous times and were now owned by various trusts established in states where getting records was extremely difficult. Jason decided he wasn't going to get anywhere that way; no matter how many layers he could get through, he wasn't going to get any closer to his goal.

Instead he used global mapping sites to look at each piece of property, and he found what he was looking for. He left his apartment and headed back to his office. Shelly met him as he was walking towards Larry's office. "Don't you answer your phone?" she asked, "he's been looking for you."

"Sorry, but I needed some time to process what I got from his daughter."

"All right, go on in. He's waiting for you."

Jason walked into Larry's office, closed the door, and sat down.

"So tell me something," Larry said, his elbows on his desk.

That was Larry's impatient stance and Jason had seen it many times before. He figured something must have happened while he had been away.

"What happened" Jason asked.

"Okay, you want to play it way, fine, I'll go first. Mallory Hill and some of her staff are in the air right now on the way to Israel and Rampling and his group of over a hundred, including nineteen Senators and Congressmen, leave tomorrow. They're using the report to their advantage and that means we need Priest. Now it's your turn, what do you have?" Larry asked.

"I'm pretty sure I know where he is."

"Did the daughter tell you where to find him?"

"Not exactly and that's the part I'm still having trouble understanding."

"What are you talking about, Jason? I need specifics."

"She gave me copies of property records for hundreds of acres of land that the family has owned for generations and there's only one parcel of land that has a building on it."

Jason knew he had to come clean with Larry: the news is by definition *new* and he felt that he needed to give Larry something that would keep him interested in the story.

"Where is this piece of property, Jason?"

48

"In West Virginia. I can leave first thing tomorrow morning."

"All right, Jason, go with it, but if you can't find him in the next forty-eight hours I'll have to shut you down. I don't have to tell you that this is a newspaper and we need to cover what the news is and you have no *new* news to write about."

"I understand, Larry, thanks," Jason said, and then walked out of Larry's office.

Jason went home early that day and once he had mapped out the route he got caught up on the events of the past 24 hours. A lot of politicians were making comments about the report but all the talking points were the same—about how we needed to show support for our friends in the region. No one seemed to have the guts to comment about the content.

Jason felt there was a problem with Senator Rampling: He was a great public speaker and knew how to rally his party, but he always communicated the same old message.

Because Rampling hardly ever generated anything new, Jason rarely mentioned the Senator's name in his columns. Jason decided to call the Senator's office; he was surprised when Ted Wilson, Rampling's chief of staff, took the call.

"I'm a little busy, Jason, what can I do for you?" Ted asked.

"I know you're, Ted. You have a trip to prepare for. I just want to ask you a couple questions and they can even be off the record, if you like."

Jason heard Ted laugh. "Off the record. I didn't think that existed in your world, Jason. Okay, ask your questions and let's call this off the record, unless I tell you it's not."

"The report, Ted. What does the Senator really think of it? I've heard the canned shit everybody's selling—what I want to know is, what does the Senator think about our intelligence agencies being in possession of and having knowledge of a report that could have saved countless lives?"

"Come on, Jason. I'm pretty sure you don't know anything more about this report than what you already ran and from what we hear, neither does anyone else—and you can trust me on this or not, but we've asked and gotten nothing back."

Ted was very skilled and Jason realized that, unfortunately, he wasn't going to slip up and say anything useful. "Okay, Ted, I can see the Senator's point of view, but come on, somebody must know something about this."

"Well, Jason, it's your job to find out, but I wish you luck since everyone who was in the meeting when that report was presented is dead. I have to run, I've got a lot to do over here," Ted said as he ended their conversation.

Jason smiled: Ted had slipped up, or maybe he just thought Jason already knew that there had been a meeting. Jason thought to himself, well, they all think everyone from that meeting is dead, but I know that one of them is still alive, and I'm going to find him tomorrow.

Jason got any early start as he was headed into unfamiliar territory: a small county in the western part of the state. There were fewer than ten thousand residents and he had a feeling everyone probably knew one another. That meant he wouldn't have much trouble finding the property.

Jason was amazed by the beauty of the scenery as he drove through the state. He had always assumed West Virginia was just coal mining country. He wondered why Emily had stopped looking for her father when she had been so close to maybe finding him. Did she know more than she had already told Jason about her father? The big question in Jason's mind was this: if he was really alive, why was he hiding? And if he was hiding, what or who was he hiding from?

Once Jason saw signs that he had entered the county, he stopped at the first gas station. The station was also a small food market and it reminded him of something from a television show he watched as a child. He grabbed his map and got out of the car. He had filled up earlier and still had a half a tank left, so he just needed information. There were a few people in the store buying groceries and chatting, but Jason paid little attention to them.

"Can I help you, mister?" Jason heard from someone to his right. It was a young man—Jason figured he was still a teenager.

"Yes, I was wondering if you could give me some directions," he replied.

"Where are you trying to get to?" the boy asked.

Jason unfolded his map and pointed to the plot of land he was looking for.

"That's Mr. Potter's place."

"That's who I'm looking for."

"Well, just head down the road that way and in about three miles you'll see a big red arch on the right side; you go through that arch and that dirt road will take you right up to his house," the boy said as he pointed a finger in the direction Jason needed to go.

"Thank you very much," Jason said as he headed to the door.

"Hey, mister."

Jason turned to see a middle-aged woman standing at the end of one of the aisles with a shopping basket in her hand. Jason looked at her and she spoke once again.

"You best be careful. Able Potter is not exactly the friendliest fellow and he likes his privacy."

"Thanks, I think he might want to see me," Jason told her as he walked out the door.

"Able Potter," Jason muttered to himself and smiled. He'd kept the initials, Jason thought, and wondered why he'd do that.

Jason followed the boy's directions, driving though the arch. The dirt road was fairly smooth but long and curvy, with large trees on both sides. After about five minutes Jason came to a large open space and an unexpected scene. He had thought he would find a small unassuming dwelling; instead he saw a huge home that looked more like it should be in ritzy ski resort town in Colorado. It must have been at least 7,000 square feet and there were a few large trees still left standing around it to give that true cabin in the woods look.

Jason parked his car about 300 feet from the house and checked his watch, making a mental note that he had found August Priest at just about 2:00 p.m. He got out of the car and looked around, but saw no one, so he began to slowly walk towards the house. When he was about a hundred feet from it an object flashed past him—a knife, which had landed in a tree 5 feet in front of him. Jason examined the knife: it had an ivory handle and the initials "AP" were engraved in gold.

Jason looked to his right, shielding his eyes from the sun; he could see a figure standing about 200 feet away holding what looked like a sniper's rifle. Jason remembered what Emily had told him about her father's dark side. It took skill to throw a knife that far with any accuracy, so Jason stood still as the man approached him. Jason got a better look, but once again what he saw wasn't what he had expected.

The man was tall, probably 6' 3", with wavy white hair that came to his shoulders and a white closely cropped beard. He was very well built and though he had to have been at least 20 years

52

older than Jason, he looked like he was the same age. In fact, he looked more like an aging rock star than a retired CIA file clerk.

"My name is Ja—"

"—I know who you are, Mr. Rells."

"I know who you are too, Mr. Priest, and I mean you no harm. I only came here to talk to you."

"If I wanted you dead, Mr. Rells, you would never have made it out of your car." He smiled. "So you must have found Emily."

"Actually, she found me, and how did you know that?"

"There is no way you could have found this place without her help."

Jason reached into his pocket and brought out the envelope Emily had given him. "She gave me this to give to you if I found you."

He handed Priest the envelope knowing that he was watching every move Jason made. "I didn't open it, Mr. Priest."

August took the envelope and put in his back pocket. He would read it later in private. "Follow me, Mr. Rells," August said as he escorted him up to the house.

As soon as he walked through the front door, Jason saw that the interior of the house was just as magnificent as the exterior. August walked into what Jason assumed was his study, and Jason followed. The study was lined with bookshelves and three computer screens were lit up—one showed images of the property, including the arch Jason had driven through when he arrived.

August open the gun case and put the rifle away and then turned to Jason. "So what exactly do want to talk to me about, Mr. Rells?"

"I have so many questions to ask you. No one seems to know what happened back then. I know there was some sort of meeting and you presented your report, but everyone who was in that meeting is dead—that is, everyone but you."

"You have the report, Mr. Rells. I believe it is obvious that no one thought my conclusions had any merit and it was filed away. So there's your story—now you can go."

Jason wasn't about to give up. Tt had been a long time since he covered real news, but his instincts were still there and they were telling him there was a lot to this story and that August Priest knew every last detail of it. "I'm sorry, Mr. Priest, but I think there a lot more to all of this than just your report and I came a long way to find you." Jason chose his words carefully as he remembered once again what Emily had told him. Besides, from what he had seen, Priest could likely tear him apart without breaking a sweat.

"What is it that you think I can tell you, Mr. Rells?"

"The truth, Mr. Priest, I want to know the truth."

August started to laugh and when he stopped his face showed his annoyance. "What does a man like you want with the truth? You're a bottom feeder, Mr. Rells, you make a living trying to destroy other people's lives. What great truths have you uncovered in your column—maybe a politician is having an affair, or isn't paying his nanny a decent wage? You once said you saw yourself as the sword of the people. What a bunch of horseshit, you have no interests except feeding your own ego."

Jason was starting to see where Emily got her personality from: her father was just as straight-forward as she was and he had done his homework, which told Jason that Priest had expected him to come here. Jason knew he was running out of time and the next words out of his mouth would have to be the right ones. You say you want the truths I have uncovered, Mr. Priest. Well, how about the truths that I do know? First, you knew I would find you, though I think you didn't count on your daughter helping me so you were a bit surprised when I showed up this soon. You could have killed me. I have a feeling that you more than what your daughter said you were— just a file clerk at the agency. You disappeared, Mr. Priest, and I know someone pretty high up the food chain had to have helped you do it because I have never seen anyone wiped this clean before. Here's the question: who was so afraid that you might be found, and who were you so afraid of that you needed to hide? You see, Mr. Priest, I followed the records that Emily gave me and the changes to the land records started to happen twenty years ago and so I think you had started this plan in motion a long time before your records were wiped out of the system. You're right about me, Mr. Priest, it has been a long time since I acted like a real journalist but I'm betting that you looked back far enough to see that I once was a pretty good one. If it is any comfort to you, I never would have found you without your daughter's help, I didn't put her name in print, and if you still want me to leave, Mr. Priest, I will. As far as I'm concerned, I never found you and you can remain dead."

August looked at Priest. He didn't respond at first but then he motioned Jason toward one of chairs in the center of the room. "Sit down, Mr. Rells."

Jason sat down and August sat across from him. "There was a time, Mr. Rells, when I believed there was only one truth but I soon learned there are many truths. Look, I can tell you this much. The supposed truth your government has told you about the Middle East is their truth and it is the one that serves their purpose. I told them a long time ago that you can't expect people who live under such conditions not to rise up and fight those they see as their oppressors and those they see as aiding those oppressors. I was laughed at, Mr. Rells, and as time went on and things began to happen as I had predicted they would, I thought maybe they'd finally pay attention to that report. Of course, they didn't and I have had to live with the fact that I kept my oath and my silence and never spoke about the report or what I had witnessed. So I live with the blood of thousands on my hands and the fact that I had given my word to someone a long time ago that I would do whatever I could to try to change the way we dealt with the people of the region."

Jason listened to what Priest said. His words were very convincing, but he couldn't help but feel that the man wasn't telling him the whole truth, and he wasn't going to get it, at least not today.

"I still don't understand why you needed to hide, and why someone wiped your records.

"There are some stories, Mr. Rells, that are better left untold and it's better for everyone's sake that August Priest remain dead and that you keep the fact that he is not to yourself."

August stood up and motioned for Jason to do the same.

"I told you, Mr. Priest, that I wasn't always the bottom feeder you seem to think I'm and I don't think for a second that you were a file clerk. If you think you can just hide out here and pretend that the world no longer exists for you—well, good luck with that."

"If I were a betting man, Mr. Priest, I'm willing to bet that the world is not done with you yet and whatever you're hiding is eventually going to come out."

"It's a long drive back to D.C., Mr. Rells," August told him as he walked him out of the house. August stayed by his side all the way back to his car and waited until Jason was strapped into the driver's seat.

Jason lowered the window and turned to look at him. "It was very nice to meet you, Mr. Potter. I'm sorry that I bothered you, but I thought you might be someone else."

August smiled and nodded his head. It was indeed a long drive back to D.C. and it would give Jason time to think about everything he saw and heard. He knew that he had no other option but to leave but he was far from done with the story or with Mr. August Priest.

In most cases, any source would keep a few facts from him or lie about one or two things. But in this case, Jason believed Priest wasn't telling him anything that was remotely true—and that really got to him. He would find the truth one way or the other, and if he had to, he would reveal August Priest's location to the world.

Chapter 8
Trick or Truth

Mallory Hill liked Tel-Aviv: the climate was great and she had always been a friend to the Israelis and their staunch defender as a Senator and as National Security Adviser. The Israeli people knew her well and the overwhelming majority of them hoped that she would be the next President. The Israelis didn't like President Garrison: In their minds, his policy on security was inconsistent and it was sometimes hard to determine where he really stood.

Over the years Mallory and become friendly with Nathan Berenfeld, who had been the Director of the Mossad for the past thirty years. Whenever she came to Israel, she stopped in and visited with him first thing. Of course, this time she had another purpose other than just friendly chat. This time Nathan had sent word that he would like to see her as soon as possible. Jim Keller accompanied Mallory to the Mossad Director's Office, though he was asked to remain outside and only Mallory was permitted to enter Nathan Berenfeld's office.

"It is good to see you, Nate," Mallory said, and she went over to give the man a hug.

Nathan Berenfeld was in sixties, of medium height and build, and had a way of making you feel like he was your favorite relative and had been looking forward to his visit. But in reality he was cunning, ruthless, and would do anything to protect the country and the people he loved.

Mallory was surprised to see that Avi Cohen in the office as well. He was the Director of Shin Bet, the internal security force of Israel. It was their job to protect the Prime Minister and to protect her and the Republican contingent that would be arriving later that day. Unlike Nathan Berenfeld, Cohen wasn't interested in being friendly. He was a man totally dedicated to doing his job. Seeing him in the office, Mallory knew something was up. She had met Cohen a few times in the past and she shook his hand before sitting down.

"What's wrong, Nate?" Mallory asked.

She had started calling Berenfeld "Nate" years ago and he referred to her as "Mal." He once told her that it took too long to say her full name.

"Do you really think that the timing was right for a visit here, Mal? It is nice to see you, but that report has got everyone on edge around here," Nathan told her.

"Perhaps Ms. Hill is fully aware of the predicament this visit has us in," Avi Cohen told her.

"Avi, please, we agreed let me handle this," Berenfeld told him.

"All right, Nathan, but you make sure you tell her everything. I'm sorry, Ms. Hill, but I'm needed elsewhere. Please listen to what Nathan is going to tell you and then go home," Avi Cohen said before he left the office.

"I know the timing is not good, Nate," Mallory said, "and that everyone thinks I'm going to be the next President, but We've something called an election and we actually need to win that in order to be President, and how could I not come when Senator Rampling and his group were going to be here? Garrison is weak—we both know that—and the American people are tired of a weak President and they're going to elect the person they believe is the strongest leader and one who will not back down on his word. That is why I had to come, Nate."

Nathan Berenfeld just sat there and listened to her and said nothing. He was waiting for what she would say next. After about two minutes of silence, Mallory realized there was something else going on.

"This is not just about Americans on your soil is it, Nate?"

"Mal, I understand that the FBI searched Neil Hawthorne's house and they recovered a great deal of information including encrypted files that were sent to the CIA and they're attempting to break the encryption."

"How do you know that, Nate? I just found out about this yesterday."

"Well, you spy on us, we spy on you. That's how the game is played, Mal."

"You're aware of my relationship to Hawthorne, correct?"

"Yes, Nate, I do remember you and he were friends, yes."

Nathan Berenfeld began to laugh. "Friends, no, Mal. Neil Hawthorne didn't know the meaning of that word. When we had mutual interests—and this is important for you to understand: Neil Hawthorne's interests were more often his own than your government's—he would contact me for our help. So it is true that Hawthorne was running his own off the books operations without government approval or knowledge. In this world that Hawthorne and I had to live in, there are many times in which it is better that what you need to do is not shared."

"You're talking about plausible deniability, Nate."

"That only comes into play if need to stay hidden doesn't stay hidden, Mal."

"All right, Nate, let's say we all have our little spies and I'm betting you already know more than I do, which is not that much, so I ask you again. Why am I here?"

"I would like you to ask the President to have the CIA cease all efforts to break the encryption codes on Hawthorne's files."

Mallory wasn't expecting that. She knew that if Nate had asked her for something as extreme as that, he must have had a very good reason. The problem for her now was that she would need to know what that reason was and she wasn't sure whether she wanted it. "You want me to call Garrison and tell him to call off an investigation because the head of a foreign intelligence agency thinks he should. Martin may be spineless but he isn't stupid, Nate. I assume you didn't think asking your Prime Minister to talk to him was in your best interest."

"That, Mal, would require explanations that I'd rather not have to make."

"All right, then. Start with some explanations—and none of your normal talking around the subject. Let's start with Priest and this report."

Nathan Berenfeld was not in a good place: he had no options other than to tell her at least a partial truth. He knew Mallory wouldn't be fooled by a complete lie but he was counting on the fact that she wouldn't catch on if he gave her a partial truth.

"Let's start with August Priest. Do you really believe that a kid with no training and no skills other than being able to speak the languages could have survived here alone for any length of time back then? Why would someone like Neil Hawthorne risk this boy's life and send him here with no backup, and no other agency contact and do so without ever telling anyone in the US government?"

"These are the questions that no one is asking because no one really wants the answers, Mal."

"So what do you think he was doing here and who do think he really was, Nate?"

"We think that he was a highly trained operative who was here to paint targets, targets that would eventually be eliminated by another of Hawthorne's off the books team. The report was a cover: why it was written and whether it was even written by August Priest is still a mystery to us."

"I have questions of my own about the report and so does the President, though I think he just wants to make sure that the blame for ignoring it is placed on the right people. I do find it very convenient that this report has surfaced in an election year and that anyone who could answer any questions about it is dead, and that you, Nate, have such a strong interest in it and that both you and Avi want us to go back home."

Nate held up his hands as a sign of surrender. "You're a very smart woman, Mal. I guess I shouldn't have tried to get anything over on you. The report is the reason they searched Hawthorne's home and the reason it is best for you to leave. All of us in the intelligence community run a few side operations, things that are done by those outside of their agencies. I know you're aware of this, so there's no need for me to explain why. Hawthorne ran what you might call an entire parallel agency on the side—the scale of his operation had never existed before. He carried out operations solely based on his own needs, without permission or any oversight from your government and against the charter of his agency—he carried them out on American soil and on American targets. If your people break the encryption, I believe they'll uncover that Hawthorne ordered the elimination of dozens of American citizens, including high ranking government officials and even members of your legislature."

Mallory's eyes were wide open and so was her mouth. What she had just heard both astounded and frightened her. If it was even remotely true, it would send shockwaves through the country.

"Hawthorne ordered the assassinations of Senators and Congressman—is that what you're saying, Nate?"

Berenfeld nodded.

"You have no proof of this, right? Other than what you believe is on Hawthorne's files. Correct?"

Berenfeld nodded again.

"You're putting me in a very difficult spot, Nate. You're telling me that you want me to stop the US government from uncovering what could be one of the biggest crimes in its history and from discovering that the man who led one of its intelligence agencies was a traitor and a murderer."

"You wanted the truth, Mal. Unfortunately, the truth is not always what we're expecting."

"How long do you think I have before they break the encryption?"

"My best guess is twenty-four hours, Mal, and if this does come out you and your fellow Americans should be at home doing what you can to restore your citizens' faith in their government."

A light went off in Mallory Hill's head. Damn, Nate was filling her head with this story about Priest, Hawthorne, assassinations and a rogue agency. It was all leading up to getting her to leave; he was treating her as if he was telling a child a bedtime story and she needed to be scared when it was over.

She smiled at him. "Not buying it, Nate. Not one word of it. I'm betting you and Avi want us gone and when I meet with the Prime Minister later today I'm willing to bet he doesn't mention anything about this. So what the hell is going on? And let's try some semblance of the truth this time."

Nate could her Mallory's displeasure in her voice. As he expected, she saw through his ruse and she would now be more open to his second story and more likely to believe it—and it was even more likely that she and her fellow Americans wouldn't leave.

"There have been rumblings even before the report came out when Senator Rampling first announced this visit."

"What type of rumblings have you been hearing, Nate?"

"Well, mostly the usual suspects, but when the report came out someone else joined in and that's what caused our alarm."

"Who are you talking about Nate and what specific threat do you know about?"

"Well that's just it, Mal—it's the Mole and we never know what they're going to do."

"You're kidding me, right? The Mole? You guys are all the same—you always need to have a bogeyman to chase. You don't even know for sure that this Mole exists, you have no photos of him, no one from his supposed group has ever been captured, and anything that happens that you can't explain must have been the work of the Mole. You want us to go home because of this. Jesus, Nate, next thing you're going to tell me is the Ghost is here too."

Nate's face went blank as if he had just seen a ghost himself and Mallory couldn't help but notice.

"Come on, Nate, the Ghost is a myth, just another bogeyman that my people made up. I've heard enough. Rampling and his group would never leave based on this and there was nothing about this in the briefings we received from the State Department, so I'm afraid you're stuck with us."

Malloy stood up and Nate stood as well. She waited for him to come around to lead her to the door. He put his hand out and she took hold of it. "Sometimes, Mal, the bogeyman is for real— that is something you'd be wise to remember."

She didn't reply, she just looked and him and then kissed his cheek before leaving his office.

Nathan Berenfeld went back to his desk, picked up the phone, and dialed Avi Cohen's number. Avi answered on the first ring. "It's done, Avi."

"I know you feel terrible about this, Nathan, but, remember, this wasn't our plan—we're just doing our part."

"I know, Avi, but she's a friend and I hope the Americans know what they're doing because if this blows up, it is you and I who will be standing in the middle of the shit storm that will come."

"I know that, Nathan, which is why we're going to need our contingency plan."

"All right, Avi. Shalom," Nathan said as he hung up the phone.

Mallory's mention of the Ghost had brought back memories that Nathan had done his best to bury. He knew the Ghost was no myth—he was the most dangerous man Nathan had ever known. He hadn't even known his real identity—only Hawthorne knew that—and he had never truly believed him when he told him the Ghost was dead. Berenfeld had a feeling that he was still out there somewhere.

Jim Keller kept silent until he and Mallory had left the building and were back in the car. "So what happened in there that was so important that Berenfeld needed to see you right away?" Jim asked.

"I have no idea but the whole thing was bullshit and I think Nate was trying to send me a message, and I have no idea why. Call our contacts and State and the White House and find out what they know about any direct threats to us or to Rampling and his group," Mallory told him.

"Will do," Jim replied.

Chapter 9
Overdue Recompense

It is virtually impossible in the modern world for any group that perpetrates crimes labeled as terroristic to survive unhindered for very long. The Mole's group was the exception to the norm. For the last twenty years it had frustrated internal security and intelligence agencies from countries all over the world. They have so far been unable to capture or identify a single member of the group that called itself "The Hand of the People."

No one had been able to stop The Hand of the People from carrying out their form of attacks all over the world. The sophistication had baffled these agencies for years. Unlike any other group, they weren't interested in presenting the bodies of their victims as a calling card. Instead, their targets were the lifeblood of a country's economy.

They had hacked systems all of the world, stolen billions of dollars, turned off power grids, rerouted transportation, and even shut down the FAA, bringing worldwide air travel to a halt for two days. To many people in government, they were far more dangerous than any group who targeted humans. The United States government had offered a bounty of $50 million for any credible information about the group, but no one had even been paid.

Abdul-Nasser was the Mole's second in command. Like everyone else in The Hand of the People, Abdul-Nasser was not his real name. He had chosen it because of its meaning: servant of the victorious one. Only he and Abdul-Wahid had ever seen the Mole and they were both waiting for him to arrive for their scheduled meeting. The Mole was the name that outsiders had given their leader but they knew him as Kasim.

They were standing in front of a street vendor's cart, talking about nothing of importance, when Kasim walked past; they both followed and soon turned into an alley and through a narrow door, which led them down to a basement storage room. Kasim greeted both men with a hug. He was about six feet tall with salt and pepper hair and beard. He was around ten years older than the other two men, who were both in their fifties

"Is everything moving along as planned?" Kasim asked.

"Yes, Kasim, and you were right—they seem to have very little in the way of a security team with them," Abdul-Nasser answered.

"But, Kasim, there are women and children as well. How are we to deal with them?" Abdul-Wahid asked.

"Don't worry: we aren't going to harm innocent women and children, they'll be released once he arrives," Kasim told them.

"I don't understand, Kasim. How do know that he is alive and that he will come?" Abdul-Wahid asked.

"I don't, Wahid, but I sense that he is, and if he is not, we'll just go to Plan B. Regardless, we accomplish our goals—that is all that matters. I'm counting on you both to make sure your parts go according to plan," Kasim told them both.

Both men nodded their heads. "Yes, Kasim," they answered in unison.

Kasim knew that for their plan to be successful they would need spilt second timing and everyone would need to do their job to the very best of their abilities.

"I still don't understand, Kasim. Why would the American President allow us to take their diplomats hostage?"

"The American President knows nothing of this, Nasser. This is all being orchestrated by their CIA and FBI and they have convinced the Israelis to be a part of it. The director of the Shin Bet is on board with this, but the old man at the Mossad is a reluctant participant. It is he and his people we must look out for. I have yet to find out what, if any, plans he has made," Kasim told them.

Once again both men replied, "Yes, Kasim."

"Remember, this is crucial to our success you must leave the guards unharmed and all clothing and jewelry must be removed from the hostages and left with the guards and the vehicles. No bags are to be taken and you have pictures of each American politician, their assistants and their families. Don't take anyone unless you have a photo. I'm certain the Israelis will try to sneak on at least one agent in plainclothes posing as part of the American group," Kasim told them.

"What about the woman—what if she chooses not to travel with them?" Wahid asked.

"Don't worry, Wahid. Plans are in place to take the woman and her assistant if she chooses not to travel with the rest of the Americans. But like all American politicians she is stubborn and blinded by her own perceived importance, she will not allow them to go without her. If all goes according to our plan, we'll capture the entire American group without ever firing a shot. Do either of you have any other question or concerns?" Kasim said, and then turned first to look at Abdul-Nasser.

"No, Kasim we're ready," he answered.

Kasim then turned to Abdul-Wahid.

"My people are ready as well, Kasim."

"Praise to Allah. Let him grant us success today," Kasim said.

"Praise Allah," the two men added.

Kasim knew this was the biggest gamble he had even taken. Over the years he had always been two moves ahead of his enemies, but this time he needed them to make the right moves for his plan to be successful and he needed August Priest to still be alive. It always amazed him how many of those responsible for the security of their countries would betray them for the right price. He had made good use of the money they had stolen from the financial institutions of the West, and that money had bought many officials and informants over the years.

It always amused him that no one had ever tried to turn him in for the ransom the West had offered, but their people were so easily bought and paid for. Today those people and the information they supplied would cause the kidnapping of the next President of the United States.

Bud Hammond had been with the secret service for twenty-one years and in all that time he had never seen anything as haphazard as the security for Senator Rampling and his fellow Republican legislators. Bud couldn't understand why he hadn't been given more men, as he had requested: the F.B.I. hadn't sent anyone, neither had the Diplomatic Security Service and the Israelis had only sent a few agents to coordinate with his team. The fact that the Israelis had insisted on planting two agents in with the group undercover and in plainclothes was even more troubling to Bud Hammond.

Bud Hammond had always been a details type of guy and the numbers didn't add up. He didn't have a large enough team to adequately protect these people and he needed the Senator to know that. He made his way to the Senator's suite and knocked on the door. They had chosen to stay at the luxurious Intercontinental hotel, which from a security standpoint wouldn't have been Bud's first choice. Ted Wilson, the Senator's chief of staff, answered the door.

"Good morning, Mr. Wilson, may I speak with the Senator?" Bud asked.

"Certainly, Agent Hammond, please come in," Ted replied and opened the door. Ted always made sure he remembered a person's name since he knew his boss tended to only remember someone's name for as long as that someone was of use to him. The Senator was on the phone when Bud Hammond entered the room, but Ted made sure that the Senator knew Agent Hammond's name before they spoke—he wrote it on a slip of paper and put it where the Senator could see it.

The Senator ended his phone call and walked towards Bud, his right hand extended, a big campaigner's smile on his face. "What can I do for you Agent Hammond?" the Senator asked as they shook hands.

"Senator, I wouldn't be doing my job if I didn't come and tell you that I don't have enough agents or support from our hosts to properly protect you, your family, and the rest of your group. I must ask you to call off this road trip today because I believe the risks are far too great and we can't guarantee your safety. I would like time to ask that a larger team be sent here to help as well as asking for more local help." Bud thought he had made a reasonable request and that the Senator would see his point.

It took the Senator all of five seconds to do just the opposite. "Thank you for your concern, Agent Hammond, be we're here for a very important reason and sitting here waiting like we're scared to be in one of our very good friend's country sends the wrong message and I have no intention of doing that. We'll go ahead as planned, Agent Hammond, and I'm sure you and your team will do your jobs as well as you're expected to," Senator Rampling told him.

Bud was taken aback but only by the fact that the Senator didn't even seem to consider anything he had said before making up his mind. He had been around politicians his whole career but their thought processes still baffled him and this one was putting votes ahead of his family's safety. "Senator, there's one more thing I've been ordered to bring along: we need to provide protection for Mallory Hill and her assistant as well. I hope that doesn't present a problem for you," Bud told the Senator, knowing that it would irk him. Bud could see the displeasure on the Senator's face at the news he had just received. The Senator didn't answer Bud, but he walked towards him. "Thank you for your concern, Agent Hammond, we'll be ready to leave in two hours." Ted opened the door and Bud left the Senator's hotel room.

"That bitch, you know she called the White House and made sure she got on the bus with us," Senator Rampling said angrily. "I'm sure you're correct Senator but there's nothing we can do. The Secret Service detail has their orders and we can't compel them to disobey," Ted answered. "All right, Ted, you start getting everyone coordinated and make sure our transportation is ready for us, I have a few more calls to make."

"I'll take care of everything, Senator, and unless you need me I'll see you in the lobby in two hours."

The Senator nodded in agreement and then picked up his phone; he no longer needed Ted and that was his cue to leave the room.

Ted Wilson had worked for Senator Rampling for almost eleven years, working his way up from a staffer to the chief of staff for the current senate Majority leader and, if all went as planned, the next President of the United States. Ted Wilson was far more of an opportunist than a true believer; he had worked for two different congressmen before joining the Senator's staff. He had left them both because he realized they would never get that far, and he had been right—neither man was still in office.

He didn't believe in what the Senator stood for any more or less then he believed in what Mallory Hill stood for—that was never an issue for him. It was his job to make everyone believe that what the Senator stood for was the right direction for the country and he did his job very well.

Ted had everything and everyone ready and waiting in the Lobby at 11:00 a.m. They had two very large custom-made buses along with three large black SUVs. Ted saw Agent Hammond's team standing by two of the SUVs and near the third were four Israelis in military clothing. Ted thought back to Agent Hammond's warning earlier that day. There didn't seem to be a very large protection detail assigned to them, and maybe Hammond had a valid point. That thought was interrupted by the arrival of Mallory Hill and her assistant Jim Keller.

Since the Senator and his family were on their way down, it was his job to greet them. "Good morning, Ms. Hill, Jim, it's good to see you," Ted said as he shook their hands. Mallory Hill leaned into Ted as they shook and whispered, "Cut the B.S., Ted, we both know this is a stupid idea."

Ted didn't reply though he didn't disagree with her—this was the Senator's idea and he still didn't know what he planned to accomplish.

By the time the Senator and his family had made it down to the lobby, Ted had everyone already on the buses, making sure that Mallory Hill and her assistant were on the second bus. He knew the Senator wouldn't want to share a bus with her. The Senator's plan was to visit different areas and show his support for the country, but he also wanted to enter the West Bank. The Israelis didn't control the West Bank nor could their troops enter that area. He had tried to reach out to those who controlled the region, but had never received a formal invitation to enter.

This was the main reason there were no American reporters allowed on the bus, and none had been given access to anyone in his group. If he was turned away he didn't want it plastered all over the news. Of course, a few newspeople had made the trip but they had nothing to report—at least, not yet.

Bud Hammond was in the lead SUV traveling in front of the first bus; the second SUV was behind the first bus, and the Israelis took the position behind the second bus. They were moving along towards the West Bank when Bud suddenly heard a rumble that turned into a blasting sound—and then road went out beneath them. When they hit bottom he was shaken up but still conscious and then he smelled something. It was gas, and he was out cold in less than twenty seconds.

Chapter 10
A Change of Plans

"Tell me that again," Kent Baggart screamed. It was just about 5:00 a.m. and he was in the backseat of his car on the way to CIA headquarters. The voice on the other end of the phone belonged to Dan Mitchell, an intelligence officer who was very good at his job, which is why Kent Baggart had personally selected him to lead the team to protect the group in Israel.

"Director, we've lost all contact with the group," Dan told him.

"What do you mean, you've lost all contact? I need some answers, Dan. I'll be there in fifteen minutes and you better have something more than what you just told me."

By the time Baggart entered the situation room where Dan Mitchell and his team were located, almost twenty minutes had passed. Dan was on the phone with Nate Berenfeld's office trying to get some answers.

"Who are you talking to, Dan?" Baggart asked.

"I'm trying to get Nathan Berenfeld on the line, Director, but I'm being stonewalled."

"Put it on speaker," the Director ordered.

A female voice came back on the line after about thirty seconds. "I'm sorry, Mr. Mitchell, but Director Berenfeld is quite busy at the moment, as I'm certain you can understand."

"Miss, I don't care what the Director is doing, this is CIA Director Baggart. You put him on the phone now," Baggart bellowed.

Ten seconds later Berenfeld was on the line.

"Kent, can you give me one minute? I'm just getting the latest news," Berenfeld said.

"All right, Nathan, I need some answers and I need them now."

"Kent, I think we should speak privately," Berenfeld told him.

"All right, Nathan, I'll call you from my office in five minutes; in the meantime, get someone from your office to coordinate with Dan Mitchell."

"As you wish, I'll wait for your call."

"Dan, for now what's going on stays in this room, do you understand?" Baggart said, making eye contact with each person in the room to make sure they realized he was also talking to them.

"Yes, Director," Dan answered.

Kent Baggart went into his office, closed the door, and dialed Berenfeld. "What's going on over there, Nathan?"

"They've been taken, Kent, and that's not the worst of it, I'm afraid."

"Really, Nathan, what could be worse than this?"

"We've a leak in one or both of our agencies, Kent. There's no other way to explain this."

"Explain what? You're not telling me a damn thing."

"They were all taken except the two agents we planted on the buses—both of them had American identification and were dressed in American clothing right down to their socks. They also left all jewelry and clothing behind as well. They didn't take the take the security detail nor did they harm them. You're getting the picture now aren't you, Kent? Do you have any more brilliant ideas, since this plan has worked so well so far?" Berenfeld's voice was full of sarcasm but beneath that he was worried that their plan would now be discovered.

Kent Baggart's mind was whirling: this wasn't the way things were supposed to go down. There was no way that whoever abducted the group could have known who wasn't an American. Nathan was right—there was a leak. The question was: Where it was coming from? "Was it the Mole's people who took them?" Baggart asked.

"Had to be—no one else could have pulled this off, no one else has this level of sophistication," Nathan answered.

"The security detail—can they be of any help?" Kent asked.

"They took a pretty good dose of the gas and they're all still unconscious; we'll speak with them when they awake but considering how fast this happened and the fact they were all found still in their vehicles I doubt they'll be of much help," Nathan answered.

"I have to go brief the Prime Minister, Kent. I really hope you two have a Plan B because this one is sure shot to hell," Berenfeld said before he hung up.

Baggart had thought he had this all figured out: he and Frank Linden had covered every contingency—there was just no way this could have happened. Kent's next call should have been to the White House but instead he dialed FBI Director Linden and informed him of what had happened.

"What the fuck, Kent, how can we fix this? Do the Israelis have any clues?"

"No, right now they're as much in the dark as we are. They believe the Mole's group abducted them, although why and what they're going to want is still unknown. Look, Frank, we're going to be called into the White House at some point today and we need to maintain a united front. For now at least we need to play this as an Israeli screwup and keep anyone from looking anywhere else—agreed?"

"Agreed. Keep me posted," Linden said as they ended their call.

The next phone call Baggart made was to the President and his reaction was predictable. As expected, both he and Frank Linden were summoned to the White House at noon and the President made it clear he wanted answers. When Baggart arrived at the White House he was escorted to the waiting area outside of the oval office where Linden was already waiting to go inside. They were both surprised because they thought the meeting would be held in the situation room.

When they went in, only the President and his Chief of Staff Robert Nathans were there. By now the story of the abduction was all over the news, though there was still no word from the group that had taken them. "Sit down, gentlemen," the President told them.

Baggart and Linden took seats in front of the President's desk. "Show them, Rob," the President said.

Rob Nathans handed them each a piece of paper. "This was dropped at our Embassy in Jordan two hours ago. Let me read this to you both so you can truly understand what a disaster this report is turning out to be. He cleared his throat and began to read: *We've your people and we'll only speak to August Priest. You have thirty-six hours to get August Priest to your Embassy in Israel. Failure to comply will mean you will never see your countrymen again.*" Nathan looked up. "It's signed The Hand of the People."

"So let's try this once again: what do we know about August Priest?" the President said, pounding his fist on the desk.

"We've not been able to determine whether he's alive or dead, Mr. President," Frank Linden answered.

"What about the files you found at Neil Hawthorne's house? Were you able to break the encryption?" the President asked.

"We're still working on it, sir," Baggart told him.

"Well, work faster! There might something in there that can lead us to this man Priest," the President told him. "Frank, what about Rells? What did your people find out? Does he know anything?"

"Mr. President, as I told you earlier, all Rells had was a copy of the report; he hasn't written anything else regarding the report or Mr. Priest," Frank Linden answered.

Rob Nathans kept quiet but he knew that Linden wouldn't have listened to the President and assigned someone to watch Jason Rells, so he took matters into his own hands even though he had broken the law to do so.

"Mr. President, that may not be entirely true," Nathans said.

"What might be entirely true, Rob?" the President asked.

"Well, Mr. President, I had a feeling that Director Linden might think that if his people couldn't find August Priest, well, then how could a reporter? So he wouldn't assign anyone to watch him. So I took it upon myself to have his cell phone tracked."

"You what?" the President said.

"I realize what I did, sir, but Jason Rells went to West Virginia and I was able to determine that he went to a property, a property whose ownership someone had gone to a great deal of effort to hide. The man who lives on that property is named Able Potter, and he didn't exist prior to the year two thousand."

Normally, Frank Linden would have argued the fact that he hadn't followed the President's suggestion, but he figured it was better to have been guilty of not listening than to have the President asking questions he couldn't answer, at least not without being implicated in a much greater offense.

As for Baggart, he was already starting to come up with another plan to fix the situation. If Priest was indeed alive he would need to be convinced to be a part of it. He too was pleased that the President's attention, at least for the moment, was on finding Priest.

"All right, Rob, give Frank the address Rells went to and we'll discuss how you got it once we get our people back. Frank, you get your men out there right away. I want Priest here if he is still alive. Kent, I want that encryption broken, I want to know what Hawthorne knew and if there is information about this man Priest. Jesus, we don't even have a photo of this man—if he is dead or unwilling to help, we'll need to send them someone who looks like him and we can't even do that with what we know."

"Well, Mr. President, if we don't know what he looks like, then the hostage takers can't know either—that might help us at some point," Baggart answered.

The President just looked at the two men and they both knew it was time to leave his office, so they got up.

"One more thing, gentlemen. We received a second communication from the kidnappers saying they'll release the women and children unharmed as soon as they can verify that August Priest is in Israel," Rob Nathans told them.

Both men were anxious to leave the President's office so they merely acknowledged the additional information with a nod. They both knew that for the moment they had dodged a bullet.

Once they were out of the building, Frank Linden checked his cell phone and, per the President's order, he had received a text with the address in West Virginia. He made a mental note to himself that if he managed to survive this shit storm he would pay back Rob Nathans: the little bastard had made a fool of him in front of the President and he could see how much it had pleased him.

Kent Baggart had other things on his mind and he needed to make sure that Linden wasn't going to cave under pressure. Kent had been Neil Hawthorne's protégé and though Hawthorne had kept him in the dark about a lot, he had taught him to always think three steps ahead of everyone else. They had a good chance of figuring out the first two steps, and right now one of those steps was keeping Frank Linden from bailing on him. Frank had never been informed about the full extent of the plan, and Kent knew that he never would have gotten involved if he had known. Frank couldn't be trusted to keep quiet if he found out now, so Kent needed to keep him under control.

"Frank, listen, this is a break for us. If Priest is alive, I think I can salvage this, bring back our people and still get the Mole and his people," Kent said.

"Really, Kent? This whole thing was your idea and I'm still wondering how the fuck you talked me into it. I understand how you roped the Israelis in but I should have told you no way. You don't have to worry about me; I'm not going to be the weak link. I have no intention of spending the rest of my life in prison, so get your people to break that encryption because if Priest is dead it might be all we've got to save our asses."

"All right, Frank, I'll let you know as soon as we do, and you let me know if our man is in West Virginia," Kent told him as they both headed to their cars. Kent knew that Frank was probably pissed off and scared, but he was still solid, and at the moment that was all he needed him to be.

Kent dialed Dan Mitchell, who answered on the first ring. "Dan, listen, here is what I need you to do. Get our best people and get the encryption broken on the files that were taken from former Director Hawthorne's home—and, Dan, I need this done fast. Also, once the encryption is broken I don't want the information entered into our system—instead, send it to a secure single access point to be opened only by me, do you understand?"

"Yes, Director. Once the encryption is broken, is there anything in particular you want them to bring up?" Mitchell asked.

"Yes. Anything they find on August Priest. I want that information sent directly to the situation room. I'm on my way back there from the White House right now."

Mitchell knew better than to ask the Director any questions—he wouldn't have answered anyway, so he just did as he was ordered.

After he finished speaking to Baggart, the first call Linden made was to Tucker Henderson, the Assistant Director of the FBI. Tucker and three other men were waiting for him outside his office, and they filed in as soon as he arrived. Linden sat down at his desk and the other four men remained standing.

"Director, these are agents Blunt, Gavin, and Anderson," Henderson said. The men approached Linden as if they were going to shake his hand, but Frank's tone stopped them in their tracks. "I'm afraid we don't have time for pleasantries. I'm sure you by now you know about the events in Israel."

"Yes, sir," the three agents answered almost in unison.

"Your assignment is to bring back a man who might be able to help retrieve our people. Which one of you is the chopper pilot?"

Agent Kevin Gavin stepped forward, "I am, sir."

"You're not to leave the chopper unless I give you a direct order—do you understand?" Linder told him.

"Understood sir," Gavin replied.

Frank Linden was no fool. If, as Rob Nathan claimed, Jason Rells had tracked down Priest, why hadn't he written about it? Linden figured there were two possible explanations: either he hadn't found Priest or he had and Priest had given Rells a very good reason why he should keep quiet about his discovery. Either way Frank wanted to err on the side of caution he had no idea what he was sending these men into.

"You are to come back here with a man named Able Potter, and this man is not to be treated as a criminal and he is not to be harmed in any way," Linden told them.

"What if Mr. Potter refuses to come with us?" Agent Blunt asked.

"You're to tell him it is a matter of National Security at the highest level and if he's still reluctant I'll speak with him directly—if necessary we'll patch him directly to the White House," Linden told them.

The three FBI agents stood up straighter and opened their eyes wider. They realized that this assignment was far more important than they had first thought.

"Are there any further questions?" Linden asked.

"No sir." Once again the three agents answered almost in unison.

"All right, get going. I'll be monitoring you in the communications center." He turned to Henderson. "Tucker, I need to speak with you. Please sit down," Linden said.

The three men left the room and closed the door behind them.

"What happened over there, Frank? Why wasn't there better security—we didn't have a large enough security contingent for the group," Henderson said. He was forty-four and had had only one job since college—the only job he had ever wanted. He often told people that he was born a FBI agent. His father had been an FBI agent and his grandfather had been a Prohibition agent, an honest one—at least, according to Tucker Henderson.

"I'm still not sure, Tucker, but for the moment we need concentrate on the task the President has given us," Frank answered. Frank was aware that Tucker Henderson was a by the book kind of guy and a very good investigator. He didn't want to make Henderson suspicious so he quickly changed the topic and evoked the President's name as a distraction.

"Who is Able Potter and why are we being sent to retrieve him?" Tucker asked.

"Able Potter is August Priest—at least, that's what we're assuming at the moment. The Hand of the People is the group responsible for taking our people hostage, and they'll only speak to August Priest about their release. We've got less than thirty-two hours to get Priest to Israel. They'll release the women and children once they're assured that Priest is in Israel."

"Holy shit, Frank, what if this Able Potter is not August Priest. What do we do then?"

"I wish I had an answer to that question, Tucker, but I don't."

Linden and Henderson were both in the Communications Center as the chopper closed in on its destination. They had patched in Baggart, who was now back at the CIA in the situation room with Dan Mitchell's team.

"Sir, we've arrived and are on the ground," they all heard.

"Agent Blunt, you have a go," Tucker Henderson told them.

Marcus Blunt thought very highly of himself and wasn't shy about letting others know it. He saw himself as an invincible warrior and still daydreamed about being a super spy. "Yes sir, we'll let you know as soon as we locate Mr. Potter," Blunt answered.

"Director Baggart, there is something you need to see," Dan Mitchell said with unusual urgency in his voice.

"Not now, Dan" Kent Baggart said.

"I'm sorry, sir, but you need to see this now," Mitchell said as he stood up and pointed to his monitor.

Baggart walked over and looked at Dan's screen. "Oh my God," he said. "Frank, get your people the hell out of there now!" he yelled.

"What?" Linden answered.

"August Priest is the Ghost—get them out of there!" Baggart answered.

Just like everyone in the intelligence community, Frank had heard the stories of the Ghost, but he had always believed they were just stories. "Agent Gavin," he said, "this is Director Linden. What's your status?"

"Hello, Director Linden. I'm afraid Agent Gavin can't come to the phone right now," a voice answered.

No one from either the FBI or the CIA spoke for over a minute. Finally, Baggart spoke up. "Priest, or should I call you the Ghost? This is CIA Director Kent Baggart."

"You can call me whatever you like, but why are there armed men and an FBI chopper on my property?" Priest replied.

"This is Director Linden. Mr. Priest, are my agents still alive?"

"Yes, they're alive, but are not conscious at the moment. I'm sure you know by now that I could just as easily have killed them. I ask you once again: why are they here?"

"Are you aware of what happened in the Middle East?" Frank Linden asked.

"Yes. But what does that have to do with me?"

"The group holding our people will only talk to you. We've been given a deadline and we now have less than thirty hours to get you to Israel. Once you arrive the group has promised to release the women and children."

"Why me? I have no authority to grant any demands they might make."

"This is all we know. We need your help, Mr. Priest. Your cooperation can at least guarantee the safety of the women and children."

Once again there was silence on the line. "All right, I'll help you but I have a couple of conditions before I come in," August said.

"What are they?" Frank Linden said.

"First, I want Jason Rells to accompany me—I want him there when I arrive. Second, you must have found Hawthorne's private files and broken his encryption. I want those files," August told them.

Kent Baggart signaled to Mitchell to cut the microphone feed, and Mitchell nodded when it was done. "How long was the FBI team on the ground before Priest came on the microphone?" Baggart asked.

Mitchell turned to his computer screen and then back to Kent. "Only six minutes and twenty-one seconds."

"Get the mic back, Dan," Kent told him. "Mr. Priest, Frank Linden again. You're asking us to allow a journalist into a hostage situation and we can't possibly allow that."

"Well then, in forty-eight hours Jason Rells will write a story about how you two assholes allowed the deaths of the American hostages, including the next President of the United States. Good luck explaining that one," August told them.

"Priest, this is Kent Baggart. Please give us five minutes to talk this over."

"All right, but if you don't agree in ten minutes, I'll leave your men tied up here and I'll disappear, and I guarantee you, you will not find me in time to save anyone."

"Frank, we need to talk in private," Baggart said. The two left the room and found a private place to speak. "Are you actually suggesting we let Jason Rells in on this, Kent?" Frank said.

"Frank, how good were those agents?"

"What does that matter?"

"He took them out in less than seven minutes, Frank, and he's at least twice their age: that guy is our way out."

"How is he our way out, Kent?"

He is the fucking Ghost, Frank, and obviously, he hasn't lost his ability, so I figure he won't mind killing a few terrorists for us. Besides, neither he nor Jason Rells is going to make it back alive—they'll die trying to gain the release of the hostages," Baggart told him.

"I like it, Kent, and we save women and children as a bonus."

Baggart and Linden returned to the room. "We agree to your terms, Mr. Priest," Linden said.

"Mr. Priest, this is Kent Baggart. Director Linden will handle things here, and I'm going ahead to Israel to meet you at our embassy. I'll make sure the files are sent to Director Linden right now."

"Does that work for you, Mr. Priest?" Linden asked.

"We've got a deal," August answered.

Baggart muted the call again as Mitchell posed a question. "Director, we still don't know what exactly is on those files, so how can we just turn them over?" Mitchell asked.

"Relax, Dan. Make a copy and bring it to me before you have them sent over to the FBI. We're not going to turn them over, not to just anyone," Baggart answered. He knew there would likely be a great deal of information on those files, information that he knew his old boss had used to stay in his position and that had made him untouchable. He would store the files in his home safe, since he needed to stop there before he got on the plane to Israel.

Baggart restored the connection. "Mr. Priest, do you need us to send another chopper to bring you back?" Frank Linden asked.

"No, I'll load your team in this one and fly it back myself. You can give me the coordinates once I'm airborne, and make sure when I arrive at FBI headquarters that both Jason Rells and those files are there," August answered.

"All right, Mr. Priest, it will be done," Linden answered.

Baggart smiled. He was going to have the Ghost under his control, just like his mentor Neil Hawthorne had done. How ironic, he thought: everything they were doing was leading up to implementing project WHITEOUT, a plan that August Priest had come up with thirty years ago, and Priest would be the trigger that would start it all. He was very full of himself at that moment, and poor Frank, he had no idea what he had really signed up for.

Chapter 11
Whose Truth Is It, Anyway?

Suddenly, Jason Rells felt useless. Everyone was calling their contacts to try to get any tidbit of information about what had happened to the group of Americans in Israel, but no one could get confirmation of anything at this point. Jason didn't exactly have any contacts in the government or the intelligence community, so all he could do was sit and watch.

But he could see that there were two men in suits heading right for him. Jason stood up and began walking towards Larry Molson's office and when the men changed direction, Jason had a feeling they had come for him.

"Mr. Rells, I'm special agent Thomas Grant, and this is special agent Brooks. We're here to bring you to FBI headquarters," the man on Jason's right said. Both men held up their badges for Jason to see. Larry Molson, who was looking out the window of his office, noticed this action and came outside. "What's going on here?" Molson asked the two agents.

"Sir, we're here to escort Mr. Rells to FBI headquarters," Agent Grant said.

"Do you have a warrant? Why do you need Mr. Rells—what has he done?" Molson asked.

"Sir, I was told that this is a matter of National Security, and I must insist that Mr. Rells come with us. Please don't interfere," Agent Grant said.

"Larry, it's okay. I'm certainly no help to you here, so I'll go with them. I don't think these guys are planning to harm me—are you, fellows?" Jason asked, trying to inject a little humor to cut the tension.

"All right, Jason, you do what you think is best." Larry motioned to his assistant, Shelly, to come out to join them. When she arrived, he told her to write down the agents' names. "I want to know who they are, just in case," Larry said. Both men showed Shelly their badges before they left with Jason.

Frank Linden was sitting in his office when the call came in from the White House: it was Rob Nathans on the line. "I'm returning your call, Frank. The President is on the line with the Israeli Prime Minister. We're trying to piece together what happened over there, and I hope you have some good news for us," Nathans said.

"We've found August Priest, Mr. Nathans, and he's on his way to my office right now. He has agreed to go to Israel with conditions that we had no choice but to accept," Linden told him.

"Conditions—what conditions, Frank?"

"We had to agree to allow Jason Rells to go along with him."

"My God, you agreed to this without consulting the White House? What were you thinking?"

"Mr. Nathans, have you ever heard of the Ghost?"

"You mean that guy who you intelligence people made up to scare everyone? Sure, but what does this have to do with Jason Rells going along?"

"The Ghost is real, Mr. Nathans. Kent's team broke the encryption, and August Priest is the Ghost. He incapacitated the three-man team I sent in to bring him back here in less than seven minutes, and he gave us no option but to agree to his terms. He said he would disappear and we would have no chance of getting him back in time to save the hostages."

"This just keeps getting better, Frank. So now we're going to send a killer to bring back our people alive?"

"It would appear so, Mr. Nathans. Kent is on his way to Israel right now to get things ready."

"All right, Frank, I'll inform the President as soon as he's off the line—but Frank? No more deals without the President's approval. Got it?"

"Yes, Mr. Nathans" Frank said as he ended the call. Frank decided to leave out the part about giving Hawthorne's files to Priest: the little shit didn't need to know that right now.

"Director, Tucker Henderson is here with our guest," Frank heard his assistant say through the speaker phone. He pushed the button to reply. "Send them in."

Linden was a bit surprised when he saw the man who entered his office. He was big, well-built, and though he had to be much older than Frank, he looked younger. If not for the white hair and beard he could have passed for forty—amazing, Frank thought to himself. He also knew how dangerous this man was and that make him just a bit uncomfortable. "Mr. Priest, it is a pleasure to meet you," Frank said, extending his hand.

"Let's cut the pretend pleasantries, Director, we both know this is no pleasure for either of us. Where are the files and where is Rells?" August said.

Frank took a large manila envelope off his desk and handed it to August. "Assistant Director Henderson will take you to Mr. Rells right now," Frank told him.

"I don't want anyone listening in when I speak with Mr. Rells—are we all clear on that?" August said.

"As you wish, Mr. Priest," Linden replied.

Priest left the Director's office with Tucker Henderson leading the way.

Jason Rells was driven to FBI headquarters without a word of explanation, and was escorted into a meeting room with a large table. The two agents who had delivered him stood outside the door to make sure he didn't leave.

When the door opened, he was very surprised to see Priest.

"Hello Jason, I can see by the look on your face that you're surprised to see me again," August said to him.

"Yes, you could say that. Do you know what's going on? Why am I here, and for that matter, why are you here?" Jason asked.

"You're here because I asked them to bring you here, and I'm here because things are not always as simple as they seem," August said.

Jason had no idea what the fuck Priest was talking about. "You're going to need to be a little clearer—I'm not quite getting what you mean."

"You can call me August, Jason. Since I'm going to ask you to put your life at risk and come to Israel with me to try to save the hostages. It appears they'll only speak with me and they have given our government a deadline for when I must arrive in Israel. Once I get there they'll release the women and children they're holding. It will likely be the story of a lifetime but before you agree to go along I think you deserve to know the truth. Even though you can never print it, you still need to know."

Jason still had no idea what was going on, but he knew Priest was right about one thing—it would be the story of a lifetime. "What do you know about what happened in Israel, August?"

"Right now I only know what I have told you. CIA Director Baggart is going to be meeting us— that is, if you decide to come along. I'm sure we'll learn more once we arrive."

"You told me there are some stories we're better off not knowing , August, so why tell me now?"

"I think you'll find out the answer to that in time, Jason, and you'll have to make up your own mind about what kind of man I am."

"I'm listening and I assume I don't have much time to decide whether I'm going to go with you."

"I did go to the Middle East in the late Sixties. I was young and I was naïve about many things and I was also very talented at certain things. I was what you would call a natural when it came to weapons—hand to hand combat—and I caught the eye of a man named Neil Hawthorne, who was heading up a new division at the Agency. The fact that I also had a gift for languages made me valuable as well. So Hawthorne sent me to write a report on what future threats our country might face in the region. The thing was, though—Hawthorne already knew that the threats were there and he knew what they were. He had me write that report and then he had me present it to a group of six men at a meeting at the Pentagon. He chose those men very carefully and he made sure that each of them would find what I wrote laughable. They did. I was angry about that and Hawthorne used that anger to his advantage.

"The then White House Chief of Staff told Hawthorne to bury my report and to make sure I never got near anything of importance at the agency. Hawthorne used me to file and translate—or at least that was my cover job at the agency, and being a translator meant I could travel to US Embassies, and that served my real purpose."

"What was your real purpose, August?"

"I was an assassin, Jason. They started to refer to me as the Ghost since no one knew who I was, who I worked for, or even if I was responsible for a given death. I became a serial killer for Neil Hawthorne and I was extremely good at what I did. I was also very good at military tactics and I was given many different scenarios and asked to devise a plan of attack for each one. I found out later that the mission plans I came up with were used by our country's military and in each case they were successful. In the end, I was the bringer of death, whether it was via my own hand or via the plans I created.

"At times I was also ordered to steal certain sensitive documents that Hawthorne used to further his career and keep anyone from looking too closely into what he was doing. The other six men in the meeting that day at the Pentagon—I killed all of them. I killed people both in and outside the United States. Hawthorne was a nasty son of a bitch, Jason. He craved power and he ran more operations outside the CIA than he did using the Agency's people. He never threatened my daughter's life, but he always made sure I knew her life was in his hands."

"Why would Hawthorne need to operate outside of the CIA, August?"

"Oversight, Jason. Hawthorne hated to have to go before Congress and ask them for anything, and he thought that Presidents were too weak to make the right calls. You see, the Agency has Black Ops teams, and when things get too messy for them, then they use outside contractors to do the dirty work. When things got too messy for even the outside contractors, then Hawthorne called me in to do the job."

"What made you stop—did you grow a conscience?"

"No, Jason. I know that probably sounds like a nice end to the story but that wasn't the way things worked out. I was good at what I did, but when Emily's mother passed away I no longer had someone to come home to, and I began to come up with a plan to make August Priest disappear. I began moving the deeds into different names and I created Able Potter—and then when the time was right, I disappeared. I knew Hawthorne would cover his tracks and make August Priest disappear and that is exactly what he did."

"But Hawthorne is dead, August, and you no longer had to worry about Emily, so why did you stay hidden?"

"You get used to a certain way of living, Jason, and though I had planned to try to become part of Emily's life, once the threat to her was gone, it never happened. I just didn't think I had anything to offer her and she was doing just fine without me. Then you published that report, which I'm still puzzled about. I would have bet that Hawthorne would have destroyed every copy of it a long time ago. So here we are, Jason. That's the story, and I have no idea what we're going to be up against once we arrive in Israel, except that I figure there's a pretty good chance one or both of us isn't coming back. The choice is yours to make, but I'm afraid you'll need to make that choice now."

"Before I do, I'd like to know one thing, August. Why have you told me all this? Since I can't print any of it, what purpose was there in telling it to me?"

"That's a fair question. If you come with me, your life will be in my hands and you may witness me do things that might shock or even sicken you. I think you have a right to the truth about the man whom you're entrusting your life to."

"One more question, August. Why are you doing this? Why risk your life for people you don't even know?"

"Do you remember what I told you when you came to my cabin? I'll not have any more blood on my hands Jason. I have to go."

It would be putting mildly to say that Jason was conflicted. On the one hand, he knew that August was right—this was a once in a lifetime story. But on the other, it was also a situation that could end his life. He was scared, but his desire to feel like a real journalist made his choice easier. "I'm in, August. When do we leave?"

"Now, Jason. Make a list of what you need. I'll make sure it is there at the embassy when we arrive."

"Can I at least call my editor? You know, they took my cell phone when they brought me down here."

"Later, Jason. We've got a plane to catch."

August opened the door to see that there were two men standing in the hallway. "We're ready— come on, Jason, let's go." Jason quickly got up and followed August and the FBI agents. They were led to an underground garage where two large black SUVs were running. One of the agents opened the back door: August got in first and Jason followed.

In the passenger seat was Assistant FBI Director Tucker Henderson. Jason knew that he was sort of a golden boy at the FBI and that he would likely head the Agency when Frank Linden either retired or was forced out.

"We're headed for Andrews. The CIA will take over from us from there, is there anything you're going to need?" Tucker Henderson asked them.

"Yes, Jason will need a few things. Give him something so he can make a list," August told him.

Tucker Henderson handed Jason a pad and a pen. "What about you, Mr. Priest, is there anything we can do for you? And the President wanted us to send you his gratitude for what you're doing."

August didn't reply. Jason made his list and handed it back to Tucker Henderson.

"We'll do our best to have these items for you when you arrive," Tucker told him.

"You'll do better than that, won't you?" August replied.

"Of course," Tucker Henderson said. Henderson was about as far from a coward as anyone could be but this man frightened him. There was something eerily dark about him. He was the human incarnation of the Grim Reaper and Tucker could sense that he was a born killer. He never turned his back on Priest for the entire trip to Andrews and he felt a great relief once he dropped them off.

Two men were waiting for them when they got out of the SUV. One handed Priest a phone as soon as they were close enough. "It's Director Baggart, sir. He would like to speak with you." Jason looked both men up and down, thinking that they looked more like accountants than CIA agents.

"What can I do for you, Director?" August said into the phone.

"Look, Priest. Normally I would be the last one to want to involve civilians in something like this but the truth is that you're probably the best trained man alive to handle something like this. What you did to those three FBI agents tells me you haven't lost your skills. So I'm going to give you whatever you need to help get our people out. Are we clear on that?"

August knew who Kent Baggart was. He had watched him when he was still at the CIA, and knew that Baggart wanted to be the second coming of his boss and mentor Neil Hawthorne. But August knew all of Hawthorne's tricks, and he decided to play along until Baggart revealed himself and what he wanted. "Yes, Director, I understand you. If you could have the head of both the Mossad and the Shin Bet there when I arrive that would be helpful, as well as the head the security detail."

"All right, Priest. See you in about twelve hours."

Chapter 12
This Lie Is My Lie

They boarded a military transport jet and were in the air very quickly. Jason sat there next to August, wondering if he had made the right decision, but it was too late now to change his mind. "You don't trust these people do you, August?" Jason asked.

"Let's put it this way. I trust you more than I trust them."

Though it was a bit of a compliment, it didn't make Jason feel any more confident that he had made the right choice. "That's not a good thing for us, I gather," Jason said.

"Look, you should stay in the background, at least at first. Don't ask anyone at the Embassy anything about this situation. I know there's a lot more going on here than we know about, and if I'm right, a lot more than the government knows either."

"I didn't realize the military had planes like this, August. This looks like Air Force One."

"You should feel special, Jason. This is a Boeing C-32, a plane that has been used by Presidents, Vice Presidents, and members of the cabinet. These seats can be converted into beds so I suggest you use them that way. We've got a long flight ahead of us," August said as he showed Jason how to convert his seat. Then he lay down and closed his eyes.

Jason's mind was too occupied with thoughts to be able to sleep so at first he got up and walked around the plane. Other than the two men who had escorted them aboard there was no one else on the plane—except, Jason assumed, the pilot and co-pilot. His thoughts went to Emily: he hadn't even told her that he had found her father and he felt bad about that.

August hadn't mentioned the note he had given him from her and he made a mental note to ask him about it. Jason didn't accept that August had nothing to offer Emily: he was her father and she deserved to at least make her own decisions about him. Then again, he wasn't exactly an expert on family matters. One thing he couldn't find on the plane was a bar—he sure could use a scotch or two, he thought to himself.

Eventually Jason made his way back to where he and August had been sitting and attempted to get some rest. The next thing he knew he was being shaken awake. "Let's go. We're about to touch down," August told him.

It was early morning in Israel and the sun was shining as Jason got up and looked out the window. "Do you think they'll have some clothing and a toothbrush for us at the Embassy?"

"In the next few hours, Jason, we're going to let ourselves be kidnapped by a group that has already threatened to kill their hostages—and your first thought is getting your teeth brushed?" August shook his head.

Jason wasn't sure whether Priest found his question amusing or idiotic, or both. The plane landed and they quickly boarded a cart that took them into a tunnel. When they emerged, two large black SUVs were waiting. The back door of the second SUV was being held open by a man who looked like a tourist. August didn't bother with the introductions this time; he just climbed into the back seat. Jason followed him in. Once they were out of the tunnel the two SUVs were met by three Israeli military vehicles, which acted as an escort to the American Embassy.

In what seemed like no time to Jason, they were at the American Embassy. It was the first time Jason had ever been in Israel, but he had a feeling that wasn't the case for August. Once inside the Embassy they were approached by three men. The man in the center was wearing dress pants and a short-sleeve button-down shirt, and the men on each side of him were in uniform. Jason assumed they were Marines.

"Good morning, Mr. Priest, Mr. Rells. I'm Henry Lawson, the United States Ambassador to Israel, and I welcome you."

Lawson was a short slender man who looked even smaller standing between the two large Marines. Jason figured him to be in his mid-fifties.

"What is the current status, Ambassador? Has anything changed in the past twelve hours?" August asked.

"I'll let Director Baggart fill you in on that, Mr. Priest. These two men will escort you to him. As for you, Mr. Rells, if you would follow me I'm sure you'd like to contact your newspaper. We've also taken the liberty of getting you some fresh clothing and toiletries and we were able to get you everything you requested," Ambassador Lawson told them.

Jason looked over at August, unsure what to do.

"Go on, Jason, it'll be fine," August told him.

August watched the Ambassador leave with Jason and then he looked at the two Marines. Probably the two biggest guards they could find, August thought to himself. Probably Baggart's show of power. "All right, boys, which way are we going?" August asked.

The two Marines escorted August to an elevator and they went down to the ground floor, but once the door opened neither of the Marines moved. They were obviously not permitted to enter the area. "Just walk straight ahead, sir," one of the Marines said. August stepped out of the elevator and the door closed behind him.

August did as instructed and when he reached the end of the hallway he opened the door and walked into a large conference room. There were three men inside waiting for him: Kent Baggart, the CIA director; Avi Cohen from the Shin Bet; and Nathan Berenfeld, who seemed to look away when August met his glance. No one offered a handshake and August was fine with that—he wasn't one for silly pleasantries.

"Mr. Priest, I want to thank you for agreeing to help us," Kent Baggart said.

"I haven't agreed to anything yet. I'm sure you've already announced my arrival to the media, and I'm sure once I was on the plane you made sure it was on the front page of every newspaper, so if these people are true to their word I bet you already have the women and children back. If they're not true to their word, then I just flew a long way for nothing and the hostages will be executed," August replied.

Nathan Berenfeld watched as August spoke. He was uncomfortable just being in the same room with him. He didn't like the idea of using August and didn't agree with Kent Baggart that Priest could be controlled.

"Well, I guess what they say about you is true, Mr. Priest. Yes you're correct that the women and children have been returned unharmed. We've kept it quiet for now. The President will hold a press conference later and make that announcement, along with your presence here to help negotiate the release of the remaining hostages," Baggart explained.

"You know, I've had some time to think about this and it just doesn't add up." August pointed first to Avi Cohen. "How many guards did you supply this convoy?" He then pointed to Nathan Berenfeld. "And you, how many guards? It's time for some truth. I'm done unless you start talking now," August told them.

"I knew this was a bad idea, Kent. I should never have listened to you. We never should have used those people, and it's going to be obvious that we did. What do you think will happen once the formal investigations start?" Berenfeld said, his voice shaking.

"Calm down, Nathan, we'll make this right," Cohen said.

"Really, Avi? Do you honestly believe that's possible?" Nathan answered.

"You're wasting my time, gentlemen. I'm having trouble understanding the end game—what are you trying to accomplish? This isn't about one group of terrorists, is it?"

"No, Mr. Priest, it's not about one group of hostages, it's about an entire region of people who are hostile to our country, to our people, and to our way of life," Baggart said.

"So you three—no, wait, let me rephrase that. I have a feeling this might be bigger than just you three. So your group has decided that the people in this region, except for our Israelis friends, are a hostile threat to our way of life and you used these people as bait, but bait for what? Let's see . . . what is there for you to gain? I can understand your involvement in this, Baggart: you think you're just like Hawthorne, and I'm guessing you just love power But you two," he said, indicating Berenfeld and Cohen. "I'm guessing you're siding with your countries' hard liners and all this talk of peace with the Arabs must be making you nervous. And Linden, you needed him to keep any investigation from looking in your direction, though I don't quite understand what's in it for him. Maybe you have something on him. So you used our people as bait, but you must have had some way to track them, or did something go wrong with that part of the plan?"

"You're correct," Baggart replied. "We had planted tracking devices on the buses and our people and there were Israeli operatives on the buses, but somehow they figured it out, and the operatives, the buses, even their clothing, were left behind."

August stood there for a moment thinking he knew something was going on and it wasn't about the hostages and certainly his being there had never been part of their plan and now they needed him, but the question was *why*. "You've got a leak somewhere, that much is obvious. They knew about the tracking devices, as well as who the operatives were—now how did they manage that?"

"We're still trying to figure that part out." Baggart told him.

"This is starting to come together for me: you didn't expect them to be taken hostage by the Hand of the People, did you? They're not known to take hostages, let alone kill anyone—they're cyber terrorists, plain and simple. You were expecting them to be abducted by a group that would have—done what? Beheaded them one by one and sent it out on video? I get that you wanted bloodshed, but why so many, why would you need that many deaths?"

"We didn't, Mr. Priest. When your report was published, things changed, and we had to deal with it," Avi Cohen said. "You see, the time has come to do something about the threat that my people have lived with for generations. Your President believes that there can be peace with those whose only goal is to eradicate my entire country. These people who believe that anyone who doesn't share their beliefs deserves to die—these are the people that the fools in both our countries believe they can trust to make deals with. Sooner or later they'll get weapons powerful enough to threaten even the safety of the United States."

"I doubt the three of you could have pulled this off. You would have needed at least the FBI to stand down, maybe even the Secret Service," August said. He was baiting them to get them to give away as much information as possible. He knew that no matter what they told him, it wouldn't be the whole truth.

"Very clever, Mr. Priest. I'm sure you've already figured out that Director Linden is our fourth," Kent Baggart said. "In fact, it was you who came up with our end game, as you call it, so it's only fitting that you be a part of it."

"Kent, shut up. Can't you see he's playing us?" Berenfeld said.

August searched his memory, but there was only one thing Baggart could have meant and he couldn't imagine they would try to use it. "You lunatics can't be thinking about trying to use Whiteout." August stopped mid-sentence. It had started to become clear to him that that had been their plan all along. He now knew this was much bigger than just four men. He looked at the three of them: Baggart had a stupid grin on his face, Cohen looked angry and purposeful, and Berenfeld seemed nervous and unsure. "So your plan is to use Whiteout, how are you four going to be able to activate it? Wait, let me guess: the hostages have all been killed and you think President Garrison can be persuaded to use it."

"No, Mr. Priest. We don't think a man as weak as Garrison could ever be persuaded to activate Whiteout," Baggart answered.

August realized then that the Vice President had to be in on it: Alan Post was an old war hawk who Garrison had put on the ticket to appease those who thought he wouldn't use force when it was necessary. "So you were going to make this all Garrison's fault, get him to resign, and then you have Vice President Post in power and he activates Whiteout. Still makes no sense—you actually think the Russians and the Chinese are going to just stand down and let this happen?"

"You think you know things, Mr. Priest, because you came here years ago and wrote your report. Well, you know nothing," Cohen said. "We've had to endure for over two thousand years of existence surrounded by those who despise us and want only one thing—to wipe us off the map for good. I'm told you're a student of military history and so you must know that there was a time when the victors would kill even the male children to keep them from growing up and taking up arms against them. This is what we live with, Mr. Priest. Each new generation is just more soldiers to the cause of our mutual enemies. The time has come to put a stop to it, for good."

"The Chinese and the Russians are as tired of all this as we are, Priest," Baggart said. "We have it on good authority that they'll be fine with the outcome; after all, the Chinese are not planning on going green anytime soon and they'll benefit from cheap oil. This world no longer revolves around politics, it revolves around business. In the end, everyone would have gotten what they wanted—that is, until your report was released and The Hand of the People abducted our people."

August finally got it: this was one big hostile takeover and whoever was really running it was pretty clever—they were giving everyone what they wanted. Whiteout would destroy all the countries hostile to the Israelis and at the same time remove those hostile to the US. Whatever countries or governments they allowed to continue to exist would be so fearful of harboring anyone seen as a terrorist that they would finally get rid of them on their own. August wasn't sure about the Russians or the Chinese and he wasn't sure any of the others knew either. "So, basically, your plan went to shit and now you need me to clean things up for you. You think The Hand of the People knows about your plan and you need to make sure none of them live to tell anyone about it," August said.

"We're wasting time, Kent—just tell him what he needs to do," Avi Cohen yelled out.

"All right, Mr. Priest. We all know who and what you are: I've read Hawthorne's files on you and I know about your daughter. This is what you're going to do for us, and once you do it, your daughter will be safe. I'll have no further use for any information about you that was in Hawthorne's files," Kent Baggart said.

August's first thought was to kill all three of them, leaving Baggart for last so he could kill him slowly, but he held his composure and showed no emotion at all. The time for killing would come, he thought to himself. "What do want me to do?" August asked.

"They must have the capability to locate our tracking devices, so we want to implant an inactive device in your inner thigh; when you activate the device you'll have three minutes to get clear before our drones fire their missiles," Baggart said.

"And the hostages?" August asked.

"Of course, if you believe you can somehow get them to release them, go ahead and try, but we're not hopeful that's going to happen. Your mission, Mr. Priest, is to make sure that the Mole and his people don't come out of this alive," Baggart said.

"So you're willing to sacrifice the life of the next President of the United States so you can all get rich," Priest said. "Hawthorne would have been proud of all of you. I'll clean up your mess but I'll do my best to get those people out of there before I activate the tracker. One more thing: don't put any devices in the newsman's equipment. If they find anything they'll probably kill him immediately and if that happens I may decide not to activate your tracking device. Also make sure starting immediately that all local news sources report that Jason Rells, famed American journalist, is here with me."

"Agreed," Baggart replied. He knew that Nathan was right; he couldn't control August Priest, it was unlikely that the hostages' lives mattered to him and there was no guarantee he would actually activate the tracker, so they would have to ensure that it could be activated remotely. He had come too far to let his plan far apart and he was going to take great pleasure in watching those who had burned the flag he defended take their last breath. They all wanted to go to their god—well, he would gladly send all of them home to their maker.

August knew that they needed the hostages to die and that they likely had another plan in place to assure that result. He also knew that neither he nor Jason were supposed to live. They couldn't allow that to happen—not after everything they had just revealed to him.

Chapter 13
Who Really Took the Bait?

The Ambassador led Jason to one of the Embassy's guest quarters. The room was nicer than many of the hotel suites he had stayed in. The first thing he did was sit down at the desk and call Larry Molson. As always, Shelly answered his phone.

"Shelly, it's Jason. I need to speak with Larry right now."

"Shit, Jason. Larry is really pissed off at you. We've been trying to reach you but your phone is turned off. August Priest is in Israel and the President has called a news conference an hour and a half from now, you better get in here as fast as you can."

"That's going to be a little hard to do. I'm in the American Embassy in Israel with August Priest."

"What? Hold on, I'll get Larry right now."

Jason waited on hold for a minute until Larry came on. "Repeat this to me—you're where?"

"I'm in Israel at the American Embassy with Priest. The FBI agents took me to their headquarters and Priest was waiting there for me. He asked me to come here with them. Larry, I'm going with him when he goes to meet the kidnappers."

"Holy shit! Jesus, how the fuck did that happen?"

"Long story, and I don't have much time. We just got here and I need to shower and check the equipment they got for me. I'm not sure how much time we have before we leave the Embassy."

"Do you know what the President is going to say? Does he know you're with Priest? You must know something—hell, Jason, you're fucking there."

"Larry, I was in a room in FBI headquarters and they took my phone. Priest comes in and says he wants me to come with him, and I said yes. They put us on a plane, we land in Tel-Aviv, they bring us here, Priest goes to meet with the CIA Director, they put me in a guest room, and I call you. This is all I know for now, but imagine what I'll write when this is over."

"Fair enough, Jason. Just keep your big mouth shut and don't get yourself killed. I want that story."

"Thanks for caring so much, Larry. I love you too," Jason said as he ended the call.

Jason was a freaked out when he opened the small suitcase they had left on the bed for him. The clothes were not only the right size, they were very much like what he had in his own closet. The underwear was the same brand he wore and so was the shaver, shaving cream, and deodorant. The only way they could have known was to have been in his house, or to have hidden cameras in there. He made another mental note to check that when he got back. He showered, shaved and changed clothes.

When he was finished he checked the bag with the equipment he had requested, and much to his surprise, everything he had asked for was there. He grabbed the bag and left the room.

Once again he was surprised to find that no one guarding his room—he had expected that after what had happened at FBI headquarters. He didn't have to wait long before he was approached, this time by an Embassy guard and a young woman in casual dress. She a long brown hair pulled back in a ponytail, and she was wearing a bit too much perfume for Jason's taste. She was neither attractive nor unattractive, and Jason thought that might have been her goal: not be thought of as either.

"Mr. Rells, my name is Denise Vincent. I'm with consular affairs and if you'll follow me I'll take you to the cafeteria; the Ambassador thought you must be hungry after your trip."

Jason was hungry—not that it mattered. He didn't think the Marine was there for his great conversation skills, it was their way of telling Jason he should go eat now. "Thank you, Denise. I am hungry and some coffee would be great as well," Jason replied as he followed them to the cafeteria.

August didn't bother to shower; he just splashed water on his face and brushed his teeth. He had no idea how much time they would have before they got further instructions from the kidnappers, and he wanted to read whatever they had on the Hand of the People. He had to admire them for their operational skills—they were remarkable planners. The one thing that bothered him, though, was that while they had stolen money, shut down power plants, even hacked government agencies, they had never once killed anyone.

Why would they suddenly take hostages and threaten life, and why had they let the women and children go when he had arrived? They were certainly worth more than his presence, and they could demand much more for their return. By the time he had gone through the files, August had more questions than answers. One thing he did know: he was going to need their help to make sure everyone, including the hostages, got of this alive.

The tracking device was inserted in the back of his thigh; it was designed so he would have to grab the skin on both sides of his thigh and push hard to activate it. He still didn't trust Baggart or the Israelis—their original plan was foolish and poorly designed and he didn't think any of them were that stupid, unless they were truly desperate.

One thing he was sure of: whoever was really behind all this wasn't going to give up if this plan failed; he would have to find all of them and kill them at some point. Almost three hours had passed since August and Jason had entered the Embassy. August was finishing up with the files when Kent Baggart came into the room.

"We heard from them—and here, give this to the newsman," Baggart said, tossing August a small knapsack.

August caught the knapsack and then followed Baggart out of the room. "Is Jason ready?" August asked.

"Yes, he is being brought to meet us right now. And nice move on the report about Rells—their note mentioned both of you."

"Where?" August asked.

"The Mahane Yehuda market— do you know it?"

August hadn't been there in almost fifty years, but it made sense as a location: midday it would be very crowded and difficult to pinpoint anyone. "No, I don't," August told him.

Priest, Baggart and two embassy guards came up the elevator to the main floor and then walked toward the front entrance. August saw Jason waiting for them along with a young woman and another Embassy guard.

Jason noticed that August was carrying a backpack. "August, I already have a bag, and I don't need that."

August tossed him the bag. "Yes you do. Take everything out of the other bag and use this one. I'll explain later."

While Jason switched bags, August turned to Baggart. "If you or the Israelis put surveillance on us, they're going to know it and it will be a waste of time. I doubt we're going to get a second chance. They can only hold these people so long before the threat of being discovered outlives their usefulness. You do know that?"

"I may not have you field experience or training, Priest, but I understand what's important and how to achieve it," Baggart answered.

Jason and August got into the car that was waiting out front and drove through the Embassy gates. Their driver was an Israeli named Meyer who Jason found very entertaining, a cheerful man in his early thirties who was very talkative. To August he was an annoying little shit who was probably Mossad and who babbled as way to get them to reveal to the Israelis something they didn't already know.

"They picked a good time of day for you to go the Shuk—traffic is not so bad this time of day," Meyer said

"The Shuk?" Jason asked.

"It is what we call the market, my friends," Meyer answered.

August looked out as they drove; he wasn't in the mood for conversation, and his mind was harkening back to the time he had spent here so many years ago. He had been a different man back then, a good man. He had believed in right and wrong back then and had known the difference between the two.

He had made a promise, one he had not been able to keep, to try to help undo a long-standing wrong, and he had never forgotten that. Being back here now brought it all back to him as if it had happened yesterday. He was even beginning to feel some remorse about using Jason, though he was a fool, but there was something likable about him. August saw him as a man who had started down the right path but had gotten caught up in the public's unending need to hear about other people's misery and the money paid to those who delivered it to them.

But Rells had kept his word and hadn't mentioned August or anything about Emily, for which August was grateful. He had the note Emily had given him in his back pocket, but had yet to open it. August had made up his own little fantasy about what his daughter thought of him and opening that letter would likely destroy that. Emily and his feelings for her was all the humanity he had left in him and he wasn't going to let it slip away.

They made it to the market in just about an hour, Meyer and Jason chatting the whole way. More than once August had thought about ripping out both their tongues, but he managed to resist the temptation.

Before they got out, Meyer wished them luck and they both watched him drive away. "Wait a minute, Jason," August said, as he pulled on Jason's arm to stop him from walking towards the Market entrance. "You do realize that we're going to be forcefully taken from this market by the people who are holding those whose lives are far more valuable to them than ours will ever be? I need you to pay very close attention to what I'm about to say, do you understand me?"

"Sorry, the smell of that market is intoxicating and I lost my head for a moment."

"All right, just get it screwed back on. My guess is that we'll be approached and led somewhere out of sight, so don't put up any resistance. We'll be blindfolded or they'll put something over our heads, and I'm fairly certain they'll drug us before they take us wherever we're going."

"Drug us? Why?"

"We'll be easier to move and easier to control. My guess is that they have the hostages drugged as well. I don't think they have enough people to keep them under control if they were conscious. Say nothing, Jason, until you hear my voice in English speaking to you. Do you have any questions?"

"No, August. I understand."

"All right. Let's go and see where this takes us," August said as they started to walk toward the entrance to the Mahane Yehuda Market. The smell brought back even more memories for August, and although he didn't understand why, it comforted him. For Jason, this was a whole new experience. He had been to all the usual resorts all over the world, but he had never been to the Middle East before today, and he never seen anything like this.

There must have at least two hundred shops located on each side of a center walkway that seemed to narrow to handle all the people walking in both directions. Jason had never seen spices in such huge containers and he saw some types of nuts he hadn't even known existed. He could hear both the vendors and the customers yelling at each other, but he couldn't understand a word they said; he wasn't sure if they were haggling, arguing, or just screaming to make sure they were heard. He made a mental note to explore other parts of the world and not just beach resorts.

Jason kept looking in every direction, trying to see as much as he could of the market. He saw a man walk past August and then turn to speak in his ear. August stopped and Jason came closer. "Follow me, we're going to go get some bread." August knew exactly where he was going and in a few minutes they were standing in what Jason figured passed as bakery at the market.

The bread, which came out of a stone oven, was round but not flat—it wasn't a tortilla, nor did it did look like any pita Jason had ever seen. The baker just looked at them before handing Jason a loaf and then turning toward the rear of the shop. He saw a door covered with a decorative curtain. August nodded at Jason and they both walked towards the doorway.

Jason took a bite of the bread: it was warm and moist and a bit sweet, and it was best bread he had ever eaten. As soon as they both were behind the curtain, Jason felt two men grab him, put a bag over his head, and then lead him downstairs. He felt a needle go into his neck and the last words he heard were August saying something in what he thought must have been Arabic.

Chapter 14
Remember Me Always

Jason woke in a fog, lying on his side with his hands bound behind his back and his head still covered. He had no idea how long he had been unconscious or whether he was alone. He remembered what August had told him and he didn't speak a word. Instead he coughed a few times and let out a slight moan. "I see you're awake, Jason, and you remembered what I said."

"August how did you know exactly what they would do?"

"Because it is what I would do, Jason."

"Are we in danger?"

"I don't think they brought me all this way to kill me, Jason, and they invited you along, so I think we're pretty safe, at least at the moment."

"August is right, Mr. Rells. My people and I mean you no harm," a voice said. Jason was still groggy but he didn't miss the fact that the man had called August by his first name. Jason heard the man say something in what he once again assumed was Arabic and he felt himself being pulled to a sitting position and then his hands were free. Then the hood was pulled from his head.

Jason looked around the room. It was about twenty feet by thirty feet, and was dimly lit. He detected the strong smell of some type of incense. There were five men in the room; the light was dim and he couldn't see all of them clearly, but he guessed their ages to be between thirty and sixty. The one who seemed the oldest was sitting down and the other four stood behind him. The knapsack that Jason had left the Embassy with was on the floor in front of the seated man. Three of the men carried weapons but they were not aiming them. Jason looked over to see that August had been untied and had his hood removed.

"You're having trouble believing it is me, old friend," the older man said as he stood up and walked towards August. He stood about two feet in front of where August was sitting and extended his hand to help August up. Jason was surprised when August accepted his hand and stood up. August towered over the old man. To Jason's surprise, the men holding weapons didn't move or point them at August.

August opened his arms and hugged the old man. "Hello, Aziz, it has been a very long time."

"Yes it has, my friend, and I'm so glad to see you," the old man replied and hugged August again. When the men separated, August held him at arms' length, looking him up and down. "You look well, Aziz" he said.

"Not as good as you, August, I'm younger than you but you look twenty years younger than I do." The old man laughed and patted August on the shoulder.

"Jason Rells, I'd like you to meet my old friend Aziz."

"It is very nice to meet you, Mr. Rells, but these days they call me Kasim—or as your intelligence agencies know me, the Mole."

August started to chuckle like he had just figured out the answer to something everyone else was in the dark about.

"Let me get this straight. You're the Mole and the leader of the group that is holding the Americans and you two are old friends. Wow, that is quite a coincidence," Jason said, though he had a feeling it wasn't a coincidence at all. He didn't think August believed that this meeting was by chance either.

"What am I missing here August?" Jason asked.

"Let's see how good your perception is, Jason. Your newspaperman's instincts, if you want to call them that," August said.

Jason sat there trying to figure out where all the pieces fit, but it just wasn't coming to him. "That's going to be a little tough to do, August. I think you're the only one here with all the pieces—am I right?" Jason asked, throwing it back at him.

August laughed. "Very good, Jason, and you're right, except I believe my old friend has some of the pieces as well. I've read everything they had on Aziz—sorry, *Kasim*—and his group and they're not killers. They're disrupters, they hack into governments, companies, banks, stock exchanges, utilities and they disrupt the flow of information, money and energy. Those three things can be far more dangerous than men with bombs and guns. They buy equipment, weapons if need be, but the most important thing they buy is people."

August looked over at Kasim as he spoke and paused for a moment. "Please go on, August, I'm enjoying this," Kasim said.

August nodded and turned his attention back to Jason. "The information they gather is their tool and their greatest weapon. My guess is that they have informants in our government as well as governments all over the world. Men and women who probably have no idea whose money they're taking and who the information they supply is going to. What I'm still a bit hazy on is how they managed to get you that report. You see, Jason, that report wasn't released to you by accident—it was intentional, but how they knew it even existed is still a mystery to me." He turned to his friend. "How did you know Kasim?"

"I didn't, August, but I never lost faith that you had kept your promise and tried to tell your people of their mistakes and you didn't let me down. It did take a while for our contact to find it, though, and make sure it got to Mr. Rells."

"So you had the report sent to me, but I don't understand why," Jason said.

"Tell him August," Kasim said.

"Because we knew you would print it, Jason. You wouldn't question it, you would never think that you were being used. You see, I'm pretty sure I needed to be alive and found for all this to work properly." He turned again to his friend. "Right?"

Kasim nodded in agreement, and August continued to constructing his theory. "You knew they were going to use the Senator and his party as bait, make it easy for you to take him, and then find you using the trackers they implanted. But you didn't count on how large that party would get once the report came out, did you, my friend?"

"No, August, we had it to play it by ear, and when Ms. Hill joined them—another surprise—I had to use you. I'm sorry for that," Kasim said.

"Wait—what's going on here? Are you telling me our government let these people be abducted?" Jason asked.

"No, Jason, not our government. This was all planned by a handful of people in our government and in the Israeli government—so far, four men that I know of, but there are more. Their original plan was allow the Senator to be abducted and then use the tracking device to target a missile strike that would kill the Senator and his group and get rid of whatever terrorist group captured them for good. Of course, the way the story would be told was that the terrorists killed the Senator and his party and then *their* intelligence work killed the terrorist group. Their plan goes much further than that and is far more sinister, I'm afraid."

"Holy shit, this is unbelievable," Jason said. "I'm guessing since you knew about the tracking devices and the plants on the buses you must have someone in the Israeli immigration department. I doubt the Mossad went so as to have their people go through customs."

"How did you know about their plan? There wouldn't be any records of this on any government computer systems—oh, I get it. You hacked one of their personal computers at home. Let me guess! It was Baggart, that arrogant asshole, who would keep this on a computer file."

"You're almost too good, my friend. I have no idea how you just figured all this out so quickly but you're completely correct." Kasim said.

"Jason I would like to spend some time alone talking with my old friend," August said.

"Yes, August, that would be nice. Mr. Rells, these men will take care of you and I assure you no one here will harm you," Kasim said.

When Jason stood up, one of the four men pointed towards a door and Jason followed them out of the room.

"You took a lot of chances, Aziz," August said. "What if I hadn't been alive—what would you have done?"

Aziz looked up. "Yeah, I know. Allah provides. I have to tell you, I'm pretty impressed. I read the files—you've caused quite a stir."

"It was you, August, who taught me all this so many years ago."

"What do you mean, I taught you?"

"You remember you used to talk to me about battles throughout history? You told me that any armed conflict with the West would have a disastrous end for my people and that we needed to find another way besides violent struggle. You were right, August. When your people were attacked they lost thousands but when they struck back in anger, hundreds of thousands died. What did those people accomplish by such an act? They made your people and the world think you were justified in destroying entire countries. What they failed to see was that by destroying those countries they further destabilized this region and that allowed even more violent groups to emerge."

"We try and take a nibble here and nibble there in the hope that someday your country will get annoyed enough to ask how the nibbling can stop," Aziz continued. "August, your people are tired of fighting wars in other countries and we see the poll results—your people would rather your government mind its own business. We couldn't take the chance that your people would fall victim to one of the more violent factions within our struggle for freedom. We knew what would happen if your people once again felt their actions were justified. I had no choice but to take action to not only protect your people but to protect mine as well. I think you now know much more about what is going on than I do, August. What else could I have done?"

"You do have a point, Aziz, and I need to know if you still trust me, even though I'm no longer the man I was so many years ago."

"I'm not the boy I was back then either, my old friend. You kept your word to me from those many years ago and I know that, just as it is with me, some part of who you once were is still inside you."

August smiled, something he didn't do very often, and he hoped Aziz was right. "I've killed so many people, Aziz. I don't even know how many. I'm not sure how much of the man you knew is still standing here with you, but if you truly still trust me, I have a plan that might finally allow me to keep the promise I made to you forty-seven years ago."

"I told you, August, I do trust you. What is your plan?"

"First, you need to know something. The hostages aren't a bargaining chip—they're collateral damage. There is an inactive transmitter implanted in my thigh; once I activate it, I have ninety seconds before the drones fire their missiles. Frankly, I'm guessing it's more like thirty seconds. "And I'm sure they can also trigger it remotely, since they had no idea what I would run into when I came in here. So the first thing I need to do is remove it and have your people isolate the frequency and jam it for now. I'll need a med kit or a knife and some bandages."

Aziz got up and walked over to a shelf to retrieve a black bag, which he handed to August. "Use this. I'll give the tracker to my best electronics man once you remove it. They're willing to kill their own people, August—the next President of the United States. I could understand when they were willing to sacrifice a few but this makes no sense, and it also defeats their original plan. I underestimated their ruthlessness."

"You only know part of the plan, Aziz. There's a much bigger goal than just the deaths of these people."

"What part of the plan are you talking about? We assumed that Senator Rampling would be the Republican nominee—he is the only person who could possibly defeat Mallory Hill and he will bow to the will of your people and very likely pull back support of the totalitarian regimes that we're trying to overthrow. Also, he has not been a strong supporter of the Israelis in the past and at times has suggested their building more settlements in occupied areas, which has been detrimental to any peace process. Ms. Hill, on the other hand, is known to be a friend to Israel and she has made it clear in the past that she has no problem using your military to push your country's agenda on those who don't see things your way. Killing her defeats their purpose, August."

"No, Aziz, killing her and every one of them is the only way they can get to the next step of their plan."

Aziz watched as August sliced open his thigh with a knife and removed the transmitter. He was amazed that he didn't show any pain and kept his concentration on both the minor surgery he was performing as well as on their conversation. "The next step?" Aziz asked.

"I have been many things these past years, Aziz, and one of them was a military tactician, or maybe you prefer the term 'mission planner'—they're both the same in my mind. I was given situations and asked to determine what the best course of action would be and how to go about achieving it with minimal losses to our people. Here's one scenario I was given: suppose a country is about to launch a nuclear attack on the US. Assume this country isn't already a nuclear power but they've still managed to get their hands on the weapon. The solution I came up with is called the Whiteout protocol—unfortunately, we don't have time for me to explain it to you, but suffice it to say that there would very few humans, if any, still alive in that country when it was over. Their plan is to force President Garrison to resign after he allowed the hostages to be killed. Then, when the Vice President takes over, he will authorize the implementation of the Whiteout protocol. I know that they have support from both the Chinese and the Russian capitals, and they will not do anything to stop this from happening. They're planning to wipe most of this region off the map, and they'll use the fear of terrorism to do that, but make no mistake: Aziz, in the end, this is about greed, not about politics. I warned them years ago that their policies would create what they wanted most to avoid." August handed the transmitter to Aziz, saying, "get this to your people and have them find the signal and jam it." He added, "Aziz, tell them to be careful—if they accidentally activate it, we're all dead. You kept the bag Jason brought—there's pen and paper in there, and I'll give you a list of what I'll need. As for the rest, you're just going to have to follow my lead and trust me—I will not let you down this time."

Aziz picked up the bag and handed it to August. Then he took the transmitter and went over to the door. Before he opened it, he turned back to look at August. "You never let me down, August. We'll do as you ask."

Jason was brought into what he thought must have been a kitchen. "Please sit down, Mr. Rells. Would you like some coffee?" Abdul-Nasser asked him.

"Yes please. How is it that you speak perfect English" Jason asked.

The four men began to laugh.

"I'm sorry, did I say something funny?" Jason asked.

"No, Mr. Rells. It's just the way the people of the West view us—you believe we're all ignorant Bedouins, but I can assure that is not the case. I was educated in your country, and we all have college degrees," Abdul-Nasser told him.

"I'm very sorry—please excuse my ignorance," Jason said. The man was right: before that moment Jason would have thought exactly what he had just described—that they were uneducated and backward. If he asked the average American citizen, they would probably think the same way. Suddenly Jason realized that Americans knew nothing about these people, but that we're told they're our enemy, so we believe they are.

Jason thoughts were interrupted when August and Kasim came into the room. August was holding the bag the embassy had given to them, as well as a piece of paper. He handed the bag to Jason and the paper to Kasim. The men, including Kasim, then left the kitchen and August sat down at the table across from Jason.

"I'm sorry that I got you involved in this, Jason. I really am."

"Well, August, I said I wanted to be a real journalist again and I am. Shit, I could have said no, but my ego wouldn't let me. Who is Kasim, or whatever it was you call him now, and how do you know him?"

"His name is Aziz and he was just a boy when I came here in 1969. He helped me to understand the other side of the story, the side our government keeps from us. You could say he was the reason I wrote the report the way I did; I told him I would try to show our government the errors of their policies."

"It was him, he was the one you gave your word to."

"Yes, Jason, it was him, and for some reason I can't understand, he thinks I kept my word and he still believes he can trust me. I need to know, Jason, if you trust me."

"I don't understand what you mean, August."

"I have a plan and if it works, you, the hostages, and Aziz and his people will get out of this alive, but you must play a part in this."

"What part do I have to play?"

"You will know what to do when the time comes. There is one thing: the truth you will hear when I speak to the hostages—you can never print it. You will write a first-hand account of their rescue and you can make me sound any way you see fit, but you can never reveal what you will hear to anyone."

Jason was still a selfish egomaniac, but he thought better of saying what he wanted to say, which was, *Are you fucking kidding me? I'm writing about all of this and I'm going to blow the lid off what will make Watergate look like a tea party*. But Jason realized that for the moment his life was in August's hands and pissing him off wouldn't be a very good idea. "Of course, August, I understand."

"Look, Jason. I know I'm asking a lot of you and I'm sure you don't think it's fair that I tell you that you can't write about this, but believe me, the reasons why will become clear to you very soon."

Sure buddy, I hear ya Jason thought to himself. But he had already started running the front page headline through his mind. He would keep August's and Emily's name out of the story but the story needed to be told, people had a right to know what their government was doing. "So what's next, August, what happens now?"

August stood up and Jason did as well. "Now, Jason, Aziz's men will take you to the hostages. You have a recording device in that bag, so go do some interviews. I'll join you in about fifteen minutes." August walked over to the door and there were three men with their faces covered waiting to take Jason to the hostages. Jason saw that each of them had an automatic weapon, and he turned to look back at August.

"It's all right, Jason. They won't harm you or the hostages—remember, you need to trust me."

Jason nodded and walked towards the armed men.

Chapter 15
Almost Nothing But the Truth

Jim Keller was feeling pretty groggy, but he was able to stand up. It took him a few minutes to put together what had happened. He was in a large warehouse, or basement, and he could smell the dampness in the air. He saw Mallory Hill and walked towards her. She was just starting to regain consciousness. Jim helped her sit up and she looked at him, her eyes still glazed over.

"Jim, what's going on?" she said, her voice weak.

"If I had to guess, I'd say we've been kidnapped, but I did a count and all the Senators and Congressmen are here as well as their male aides, but you're the only woman here."

"Help me up, Jim."

Jim helped her get to her feet. She was still groggy and needed to lean against the wall at first. She looked around the room: Jim was right—all the female staff was missing, as well as the family members. "Help me get over to Senator Rampling, Jim."

Jim Keller braced her as they walked over to Senator Rampling, who trying to sit up.

"Andrew, are you all right?" Mallory asked.

"I'm not sure where we are or what happened," Rampling said.

"You were all drugged or gassed or something like that and then you were kidnapped," a voice said.

I know that voice, Jim Keller thought to himself, but it couldn't be—he turned to look and there was Jason Rells. Jim could not imagine how Rells could possibly be here and why he was accompanied by armed men.

Senator Rampling was now up on his feet and his head was clearing. He headed towards Jason and the guards. "What is going on here, Rells? I want answers and I want them now. I'm a United States Senator and I demand that these people let us go immediately," he said in a voice as loud as he could muster.

The guards on either side of Jason raised their weapons and pointed them towards the hostages. Senator Rampling quickly stepped back, almost falling down. "I'm sorry, Senator," Jason said. "But here you don't give orders, you take them. And I find it quite interesting that the first words out of your mouth are demands. How about, Where is my family, or are they safe?"

"The Senator was drugged, as you said, Mr. Rells. Obviously, he has been affected by that. I can assure you his first thought was for the well-being of all of the families," Ted Wilson said.

"Wow, Ted, that was some good stuff. Senator, you better keep this man around and give him a raise," Jason said.

"All right, Mr. Rells. Please tell us what is going on and where the rest of our group is," Mallory Hill said.

Jason had always admired Mallory; she was as no nonsense as a politician could be, and she was the only person he could actually see as the next President. He remembered what August had told him and he kept what he knew about the reason they had been kidnapped to himself, at least for the moment. "Your families are safe. They were released along with all the female aides. You, Ms. Hill, are the only female captive."

They were all fully conscious now and paying very close attention to every word Jason said.

"Why are you here, Jason?" Ted Wilson asked.

Jason thought carefully before he spoke. He wasn't sure how much the men holding the weapons would allow him to say and he was quite certain that they understood English. He turned to look at the men on both sides of him before he answered Ted's question. They made no gestures so he assumed he could continue. "The group that is holding you is called The Hand of The People. The only demand they made was that they would only speak to August Priest. They would only agree to negotiate your release with him. They agreed to release the women and children once he arrived in Israel."

"I thought Priest was dead," Senator Rampling said.

"You should be glad that he is not, Senator, but I'll let him explain that part to you, as he will be joining us shortly."

"So, Mr. Rells, you came here with Mr. Priest. Why?" Mallory Hill asked.

"Mr. Priest had his own conditions and one of them was that I be allowed to come with him."

"Why you, Jason? You're not exactly known for being interested in anything that resembles the truth," Ted Wilson said.

"That same thing could probably be said about every one of you in this room," August said as he walked up behind Jason. "What's your name?" August asked, pointing his finger at Ted Wilson.

"His name is Ted Wilson and he's with me. And who are you? Are you Priest?" Senator Rampling replied.

August was now standing on Jason's left. He reached toward one of the gunmen, who handed him a pistol, which he took with his right hand. In his left hand was a large brown envelope.

"What the hell is going on here? I demand some answers," Senator Marco Gonzalez said. He was part of the new breed of young flamboyant lawmakers. He was a Tea Party favorite and even though he was young and had limited political experience some were suggesting that he challenge Mallory Hill for the Democratic nomination. He had won his senate seat from a long-standing Republican and he proved he could carry his home state of Florida, which was a very important state in any Presidential election.

August looked around the room and then he spoke to the gunman in Arabic. All four of them nodded their heads, lowered their weapons, and stepped back.

"Mr. Rells, would you care to introduce us to your friend?" Mallory Hill said.

"My name is August Priest, Ms. Hill, though you may also know me by another name I was given over the years—The Ghost."

Mallory's eyes widened and she caught her breath. She stepped backward, almost falling into Jim Keller's arms.

"Are you all right, Mallory? What is The Ghost?" Senator Rampling asked.

Mallory Hill had been the National Security Advisor and she had heard stories of The Ghost, though she never believed them. She didn't think it was possible that one man could have killed as many people as The Ghost was supposed to have killed. She always thought he was just a bogeyman the intelligence community had made up. Then it hit her: Nathan Berenfeld had tried to get her to leave Israel—he had been trying to warn her, and he had known that The Ghost was for real. "Berenfeld, you son of a bitch" she muttered under her breath, but it was loud enough for August to hear.

"Yes, Ms. Hill, you're on the right track. All right, let me fill you in," August told them. "Jason, take out the recording device you have in your bag and turn it on."

Jason did as August said.

"Senator Rampling, you were initially the target and when you announced your little field trip over here, that is when they came up with this plan."

"What sort of plan, Mr. Priest?" Senator Rampling asked.

"To let you get kidnapped. And once you were, they would use the tracking system that was embedded in your clothes or jewelry or wherever they hide it to target a missile and blow you and whoever was holding you to bits."

"That is absolutely preposterous, Mr. Priest. You want us to believe that there are high-ranking officials in our own government who wanted us dead, and that is just not something I will believe," Senator Rampling said.

"I figured you might think that way, Senator. Here, have a look at this," August said, handing him the envelope he was holding.

Senator Rampling opened the envelope and pulled out a large stack of papers, his eyes growing wider as he read. "Ted, come here," the Senator said, and Ted came over to stand next to him.

The Senator handed him some of the papers. "How could you have gotten this information, Mr. Priest?" Ted Wilson asked.

"There are transcripts of private conversations here. How could he get his hands on this?" Senator Rampling asked.

"What you're reading, Senator, is just part of what the people holding you got off Kent Baggart's private computer. They have been watching you for quite a while. This organization—the Hand of the People—had the report I wrote released to Mr. Rells."

"Mr. Priest, what is the end game here?" Mallory Hill asked.

"The end game, at least to begin with, Ms. Hill, was that all of you would be kidnapped by a violent terrorist group and that all of you would be tortured and executed and the video of those executions would have caused such outrage in the US that President Garrison would have been forced to resign. Then, once the Vice President was sworn in, he would have activated the Whiteout Protocol."

"Whiteout? Mr. Priest, how do you even know that name?" Mallory asked.

"I know because I was the one who came up it—it is my plan, Ms. Hill. I know what it was designed for, and I know what you're thinking: the rest of the world would never stand by and let us implement it, but you're wrong. They will. So far I have been able to identify only five of the participants: the Vice President, FBI Director Linden, CIA Director Baggart, as well as the head of Mossad and Shin Bet, though I'm guessing they would have had to have someone in the Secret Service, since your protection detail was way too small for the amount of people that were here."

"I'm still not understanding this, Mr. Priest. What is the Whiteout Protocol?" Rampling asked.

"Whiteout, Senator, was designed to be used on a country that was an imminent nuclear threat to the United States. It was designed not only to destroy the capability to deploy such a weapon, but also to eradicate all life. In other words, to leave nothing and no one alive, to wipe it off the face of the world," August answered.

"Jesus, who would commission such a plan? It's barbaric," Rampling said.

"They don't see it that way, Senator. They see it as a way to accomplish two goals: first, to remove any threat of terrorism, now and in the future. Whiteout is intended to wipe out the entire Middle East, so there will no longer be any breeding grounds for terrorism. And once the rest of the world sees what happens to any country that harbors these groups, they'll make sure that they too are eliminated. The second part is the real reason they've gotten this far. Once they've destroyed the countries in this region, the US, Russia, and China will divide the oil fields equally. You see, to the Israelis, this is about finally securing their borders and the security of their nation; to everyone else, this is not about politics or religion, it's about power and greed."

Oh my God, Mallory Hill thought to herself. *Nathan Berenfeld tried to warn me off, he was trying to tell me to leave the country and go home, he was trying to save my life.* "Mr. Rells told us that you were the only one who The Hand of the People would speak to and that you're here to negotiate our release. From what I've witnessed it seems these men are already doing as you ask, so what do you want from us?" she asked.

August had never met Mallory Hill before today, but he had heard things about her over the years, like the fact that she was good under pressure, was quick to size up a situation, as well as tough-minded and very smart. She seemed to be living up to that. "What Jason told you is correct, Ms. Hill, and before you were taken hostage I had no involvement with this group at all. It was only when we landed in Israel and I was taken to our Embassy, where I met Kent Baggart Nathan Berenfeld and Avi Cohen, that I was able to figure out most of their plan," August said. "The rest I learned from the people holding you, Ms. Hill, and I'm afraid that all our lives are now in danger." August reached into his left pants pocket and pulled out an object, holding it up for all to see. "This is an inactive tracking device that was planted in my thigh; I was supposed to activate it once I had gained your release. I was told I would have three minutes to clear myself from the blast area but I'm guessing that I would not have had more than thirty seconds before this whole area was blown to bits and all of us along with it. Right now the signal is being jammed since I'm fairly certain if it were not we'd all be dead by now."

"My god, let me out of here!" Senator Rampling cried, as he tried to make his way towards the door. Ted Wilson was able to grab him and restrain him before he reached the gunmen, who had raised their weapons and were pointing them in the Senator's direction.

"Damn it, Andrew, grow some fucking balls! If we were all going to be blown up, do you think he would have showed that thing to us?" Mallory Hill said in disgust.

"Very good, Ms. Hill. Let's see if any of you have truly grasped what is going on here. You were kidnapped by a group that has never taken a hostage or a life in all the time it has been in operation. They let the children and non-essential women go when it was announced that Jason Rells and I had landed in Israel, before I even met them or they could verify that I was indeed the author of the report that was published in the Washington Post. Do any of you have an idea of what is going on here yet?"

"What are you talking about Mr. Priest? You're making no sense at all," Rampling said.

"Senator, you're a fucking moron, and I have no idea how you made it this far in politics," August said.

Jason couldn't help himself and he let out a chuckle.

"Are you trying to give me a lesson in politics, Mr. Priest? Because if you are, you're wasting your time! I've forgotten more than you could ever learn about that subject," Rampling said.

"No, Senator. I know nothing about politics or greed, or quests for power—I leave that to people like you. What I *do* know a great deal about is life and death, and right now whether you live or die is solely at my discretion," August told him.

"Oh my God, they kidnapped us to save us from a more violent group! These people knew we would have been executed if we had been taken by someone else, so they saved our lives," Mallory Hill said.

"Well, Ms. Hill, if you're not elected our next President I feel sorry for the United States, since these idiots probably couldn't find their assholes without a road map," August said.

Once again Jason couldn't keep from letting out a burst of laughter.

"Well, Mr. Priest, I assume you have a way for us to get out of this alive, so let's hear it," Mallory said.

"I have a bargain for you: I'll give you all your lives on one condition," August told them.

"What condition is that?" Mallory asked.

Chapter 16
The Pieces Fall Apart

"Shelly, do we any news yet?" Larry Molson asked. He was standing in the doorway of his office.

"I can't get anything from anyone, even tried calling our Embassy in Tel-Aviv, but they stonewalled me as well," Shelly replied.

What's the point of having a reporter right in the middle of this shit when you can't even reach him? Larry thought to himself. He decided to call in a favor—Rob Nathans owed him a few and it was time to call one of them in. He went into his office, closed the door, and picked up his phone. Larry had to wait about five minutes on hold before Nathans picked up. "Larry, are you calling to give me something or to get something from me?" Nathans asked when he came on the line.

"So you don't know anything either," Molson said. "I was hoping you were calling me because you heard from your guy. I have to brief the President in a few minutes and I've got nothing. "By the way, how did Rells pull this off? Honestly, I'd tell you if I knew but I haven't heard from him since he got to the Embassy."

"Larry, I have to run—can't keep the President waiting," Nathans said as he ended the call. He had no idea what Jason Rells knew and he wasn't about to tell Larry Molson that the fate of the next President was in the hands of the most dangerous assassin in history of U.S. Intelligence. It was going to be difficult enough to explain that to the President, not to mention to explain why he hadn't informed him earlier about who Priest really was.

The President was pacing when Nathans entered the Oval Office. "What's so important that I needed to leave the situation room?" the President asked.

"Mr. President, I need to inform you about a certain matter and I wanted to make sure my information was correct before I made you aware of it."

"What is it Rob?"

"It's about August Priest, sir."

The President stopped pacing and looked Rob Nathans directly in the eye. "What about August Priest? Rob, keep in mind that at the moment he's the only hope of getting our people out alive so that makes him a hero right now."

"Yes, Mr. President, but Priest is also something else: he is The Ghost."

"The Ghost—what's that?" Martin Garrison had been the Governor of Florida before winning the Presidency and he hadn't been privy the D.C. culture; those stories were part of the folklore of the intelligence community, and he'd never heard them.

"The Ghost, Mr. President, was the most proficient assassin our country has ever known. He's likely responsible for the deaths of hundreds of people—under former Director Hawthorne's orders, he killed inside the US as well as outside." Nathans waited for the President to react.

He didn't have to wait very long. Martin Garrison walked over to his desk and with a swipe of his arm sent the contents flying. "You're telling me that we sent an assassin to rescue our people, Rob?!"

"Yes, Mr. President."

"Who knew about this?"

"From what I gather. both Director Baggart and Director Linden, and perhaps some of their support staff."

"Does the reporter know?"

"I don't believe he does. I spoke to his editor a few minutes before I came to see you. I figure that if the reporter knew, Larry Molson would have been asking questions."

"You're sure about that?"

"Yes sir, I've known Molson long enough to realize that if he knew anything he'd want clarification from us before went to press on it."

"Get me Kent Baggart on the phone right now."

"Yes sir, Mr. President," Nathans said as he stooped to pick up the phone the President had sent flying.

Baggart was sitting alone in an office in the basement of the American Embassy in Tel-Aviv. He was on a conference call with Frank Linden, Nathan Berenfeld, and Avi Cohen.

"Kent, how did we end up putting our asses on the line with a man like Priest being our only way out? How the fuck are we supposed to trust him?" Frank Linden said.

"Relax, Frank, I have Priest under control," Baggart said, hoping to keep their little conspiracy from unraveling. Kent could only say so much, given that Linden had never been told the whole plan. If he revealed it now, he would certainly try to back out and Kent needed his help, at least for now.

"I'm sorry, Kent, but you can't control a man like that. I saw the look in his eyes—you don't have him under control," Berenfeld said.

"Nathan, we're too deep into this to back out now, so we have to do what we can to help," Avi Cohen said.

"The reporter, Rells, what do we do about him? What if Priest talked to him—you don't think he's going to print what he knows?" Frank Linden said.

"That's why I arranged this call, Frank. Rells won't make it out of this alive and neither will the hostages. If Priest sends the signal, we'll fire twenty seconds later and if there is no signal we'll activate the tracker from here in thirty minutes and fire. After that, if Rells, Priest or any of the hostages makes it out alive it's up to your people to make sure their bodies are found in the wreckage. It's the only way we can accomplish our goals. Are you all still with me?" Baggart asked.

The answer from all three of the men was the same: yes. Although Nathan Berenfeld said yes, he had no intention of following Kent's plan. He intended to make sure that anyone who made it out when the missile struck would be safe from any further harm.

"All right, I have to go. The White House is calling, probably wanting an update," Baggart said.

"What are you going to tell them, Kent? Linden asked.

"As little as possible, Frank. Now I have to go," Baggart said and he pushed the blinking button to connect him to the White House.

"Director Baggart, Rob Nathans. I have the President for you."

"Yes, Mr. President, how can I be of assistance?"

"Well, Kent, for starters you can tell me how the hell you put the fate of our people in the hands of the most ruthless assassin this country has ever produced and failed to inform me before you sent him in. I guess you didn't think that I'd have a problem with that. Right now, your judgment is in question and considering the stakes over there I'm considering removing you as point man on this."

Baggart knew he needed to think fast because he could not allow that to happen. He had to be in charge to be able to handle the cleanup and make sure there would no loose ends. "Mr. President, I did tell Mr. Nathans who Mr. Priest was and we were under a time constraint. And please note that we have already retrieved the women and children and they're all safe. Mr. President, with all due respect, there is probably no one better equipped to bring those people back safely than August Priest. I did the only thing possible under the circumstances."

"What do you mean, no one is better equipped?" the President asked.

"Priest speaks their language and they have no idea what he's capable of. If he can't get them out by negotiating he'll do it in his own way, and I assure you, Mr. President, he is more than capable of doing so," Baggart said.

"Hold on, Kent," the President said, and he muted the call. "Did he tell you about Priest, Rob?"

"Not that I remember, though a lot has been going on in the last twenty-four hours."

"Do you think I should replace him?"

"Mr. President, he's probably right and he really didn't have a choice: Priest was our only option."

The President unmuted the call and brought Baggart back on the line. "All right, Kent, get our people back, but when this is all over, we are going to need to have a little chat, do you understand?"

"Yes, Mr. President, I do, and I'll do everything I can to bring our people back safely and make sure that no ever tries anything like this again."

Jason Rells watched and listened to August and even though he was, by his own admission, a mass murderer, he somehow admired him. He was himself, no bullshit. He didn't pretend to be anyone other than who he was and he didn't need anyone's acceptance or understanding. Jason also felt something else that he couldn't quite understand: he was not afraid. That really amazed him since the odds were not exactly on his side—after the story he had just heard, he was pretty sure that the odds of his survival were not great. Jason didn't know what conditions August was about to stipulate, but he was about to find out.

"The condition, Ms. Hill, the condition is, you listen, you learn to communicate with people, not just label them your enemy because it suits your purpose. What I wrote in that report forty-seven years ago was true then—and you should realize by now that it is even truer today. That old saying, "the enemy of my enemy is my friend," means something. And so does this: the friend of my enemy is my enemy. Our country has helped breed its own enemy by avoiding the truths we find distasteful and allowing so many wrongs to go unnoticed in the name of our national interest. I watch in amazement as we chastise one nation for human rights violations while we ignore it in others because they serve a purpose.

"If that purpose is to allow a military base of one of our corporations to drill in their sand—that doesn't matter. We aren't the ones who are using them, it's the leaders of these countries who are using us. Without our support, their power over their people will disappear; you talk about freedom and democracy but only when the outcome is what you want.

"You politicians are all a bunch of egomaniacs who lost sight of your duty long ago; you no longer serve the people who elected you, you serve yourselves and the groups whose money got you in office to begin with.

"It's time to face the facts: our enemies will no longer come at us with armies that we can blow off a battlefield—no, our enemies attack us with computers and car bombs. They have no chance of ever defeating us that way and, believe me, they know it, but they won't stop, not until all of you open a dialogue."

"You want us to negotiate with terrorists, Mr. Priest, and that just can't happen," Mallory Hill said.

"No, Ms. Hill, I'm not suggesting you negotiate with terrorists. What I'm suggesting is that you start to ask yourself how they became terrorists in the first place and what we can do as country to try to stop more young men and women from becoming what we label a terrorist.

"When you go into a region and start dropping bombs and overthrowing governments, all you end up doing is creating chaos, and when the smoke clears, you've got fertile ground for even more of our enemies to grow. Would you go in and bomb Demark because they want to ban lead, or the Saudis because our attackers came from there, or China because they're destroying the environment? No, of course you wouldn't. You see, even our double standards have double standards. We're fools with big guns and bigger egos who think we can change things by killing.

You want to know where the circle of hatred starts—well, look in the mirror. What I'm asking you all to do is to finally open your eyes, take the blinders off, and see where our failed policies have gotten us. How many more of our soldiers have to die fighting wars that were started by the simple fact that we keep making the same mistakes over and over again?"

Jason was glad he was recording all of this because what August had just said was moving. He sounded more like a learned scholar teaching a class than a man who had spent most of his life killing people. At that moment he was proud to be standing there because he thought he might be witnessing something special.

"You may not be entirely wrong, Mr. Priest. I doubt any of us can say that our foreign policy has been working that well, but what makes you think that those who wish us harm would be open to a dialogue?" Mallory Hill asked.

"Maybe we need a man like you, someone who understands these people to help us reach them," Senator Rampling said.

August smiled. "No, Senator. I'm no diplomat and I'm afraid this is where it started for me and this is where it will end."

"August, what are you talking about?" Jason asked.

"One of you will become the next President. The rest of you all hold positions of power in your legislative bodies, so I ask all of you if you agree to my condition," August asked, avoiding Jason's question for the moment.

The hostages all looked at each other and some nodded in agreement, while other gave a thumb's up.

"We agree to your condition, Mr. Priest," Senator Rampling said.

"Jason, I need you recorder," August said.

"Why, August?"

"You're my insurance policy, Jason. That recording will keep everyone from going back on their word. I never really trust a politician to do what they say they will. You'll get this back and we'll keep copies of this recording just to make sure that no one thinks you're the only one who has a copy. One of these men will lead you out of here to a place where you will be recognized and where there is no chance that any military action can be taken against you. I would also suggest that all of you stop treating Jason like he isn't a real journalist. He is that and it would serve all of you well to give him the chance to prove it to you."

"What about you, August?" Jason asked.

"I'm afraid this only works if this tracking device is triggered and the missile hits its target. They'll have people waiting somewhere out there and the explosion should distract them long enough for all of you to escape."

Jason walked over to August and put his hand out, and this time August took it. "Thank you, August. I'll write a story that will make Emily proud she is your daughter."

"I appreciate that, Jason, now get out of here."

One of the gunmen waved his arm, indicating they should follow him. Jason watched as Mallory Hill walked over to August and grabbed his shoulder. He bent down slightly and she whispered something in his ear. August turned to look at her and nodded.

They were led out through tunnels and after about five minutes they heard the explosion. A few minutes later the gunman pointed them in a direction and then vanished. They came out on a busy street and, as August had said, they were quickly recognized and brought to the American Embassy, where Jason was asked to hand over his bag. August had been right about that as well: the recording would certainly never have been given to him and August had probably saved his life a second time by taking it.

Mallory Hill immediately contacted President Garrison, who in turn contacted Ambassador Lawson, who turned over operational control of the Embassy to former National Security Advisor Mallory Hill. Upon hearing the hostages had been found safe and were en route to the Embassy, Baggart headed back to Washington; he had already left the Embassy before the hostages arrived. Though his plan had failed, he did succeed in bringing the fact that the US was still in danger at all times and in all places to the attention of the American people. He would figure out a way to come out of this as a hero.

He had already received word that multiple bodies had been found in the wreckage and he was confident that August Priest was among them. He was the only one who knew about their plan and Baggart was confident that his co-conspirators would never reveal anything. He would probably have to endure a tongue lashing from the President, but he knew that Martin Garrison was in no position to ask for his resignation—after all, he was the one who had brought Priest to Israel and that decision had saved the hostages. As for the rest of the group, Kent knew they would never give up—these countries would be destroyed and their ultimate goal would be realized. He smiled to himself as he thought of that saying, "Live to fight another day."

While the hostages were being reunited with their families and the staff members who had been released earlier, Jason Rells was escorted to a guest quarters. The suite contained a full-size bed, a nightstand with a lamp and clock, and a bathroom. There was no telephone and the two Embassy guards posted outside were under orders to prevent Jason from leaving the room. Jason freshened himself up and sat down on the bed to wait.

After almost ninety minutes, the guards requested that Jason come with them. They led him to the elevator and then to the ground level of the Embassy. They walked Jason towards a door and then stopped; it took Jason a moment to realize that the two guards were not permitted to go inside. He opened the door and entered the room.

It was a very large conference room with a long table with at least a dozen chairs, though no one was sitting in them. The only people in the room were those who had been held hostage; the other support staff who had been released earlier were in attendance.

"Mr. Rells, I'm sorry to tell you that it appears Mr. Priest didn't survive the explosion that leveled the building we were being held in. We all owe him our lives and no one in this room doubts that what he said was the truth" Mallory Hill said.

Damn, Jason thought to himself, *here come the part where they want something from me.* So he decided to play along. August hadn't taken the recorder to keep Kent Baggart from getting it, he had taken it to keep them from getting it. "What do you want from me?" Jason asked.

"We realized your first instinct would be to write the story as it happened—your personal Watergate, so to speak—but let's put this in perspective. If you write the story as it happened, the truth about Mr. Priest will come out as well. And right now August Priest is a hero and we would like him to remain as such," Mallory Hill said.

"What about the men who planned this? What do you intend to do about them?" Jason asked.

"They'll be made accountable for the crimes they committed—when the time is right. And this isn't the time. We can't have the heads of four intelligence agencies, as well as the Vice President, being charged with treason; it would have a far-reaching effect on the security of our country, as well as on the Israelis," Mallory Hill replied. "If we take Mr. Priest at his word then there are others involved in this, and if we want to find them as well, we'll need to move cautiously."

Jason knew they were probably right: his first thought was to tell say that he didn't care and that he was going to write the story anyway, but that wasn't what ended up coming out of his mouth. "All right, let's say I go along with this for the security of our country, what would you have me write about when I file my story—and what do I write about in the future?" Jason asked. He had decided that he could always write the story later if he had to, because he had the tape. He wanted to see what they were willing to offer him for his silence.

"One of us in this room, Mr. Rells, will be the next President, and that person will give you unprecedented access to the White House. You will also be granted the same type of access to both the House and the Senate. In other words, you'll be the reporter other reporters come to for information. You can write what you like about Mr. Priest, though I believe you somehow admired him, which means you'll write about how he gave his life to save us, which is exactly what all of us will do," Mallory Hill said.

Jason thought over their offer: it was everything he could have hoped for. "There's just one thing I need to be clear on before I say yes. Do you intend to keep your promise to August?"

"We do, Mr. Rells, we do. Though none of us can say whether anyone will agree to stop their actions and begin dialogue," Mallory Hill said.

"Then I agree," Jason said.

Chapter 17
Washington D.C., 2017

Jason wrote his story and August Priest became a hero to the American people. He was posthumously awarded the Presidential Medal of Freedom and the Congressional Gold Medal. Emily was given both medals and Jason accompanied her to both ceremonies. Jason had gone to see Emily when he arrived back home, and they had become very close friends who were often seen together. In fact, the gossip around D.C. was that they were a couple. Jason told her that August's last words to him were for her: he said he was sorry he had never been there for her. That seemed to matter a lot more to Emily than Jason thought it would and he was glad he had told her.

The rest of the truth about her father would remain a secret. Jason had made a promise to himself that he would never reveal anything about August's life as The Ghost. To Jason, that man didn't exist. Though he hadn't known August very long, the man he knew hadn't been a killer, but instead a man who believed in what he had written almost fifty years ago. That was the August Priest he would always remember and be proud to have known.

A month after the hostages were recused, Kent Baggart died. His death was ruled accidental and the next day his house burned to the ground, with faulty electrical wiring listed as the cause. Three weeks later Frank Linden died in his sleep—the cause of death was listed as a heart attack.

A short time later Avi Cohen died in the exact same way. Jason was always amazed that no one ever thought their deaths might somehow be connected.

Nathan Berenfeld retired after Avi Cohen's death. He knew he had been spared and he lived out the rest of his life never knowing who might have spared him or why. He tried to contact Mallory Hill numerous times, but she never returned any of his messages; they would never see or speak to each other again.

Soon after, the tape recorder was delivered to Jason, just as August has said it would be. Jason had no idea how it had gotten to him but he made two copies of the recording and put the recorder somewhere safe.

Senator Rampling ended up getting his party's nomination and the 2016 Presidential campaign, as expected, was a contest between the Senator and Mallory Hill. It would become somewhat historic for two reasons: it was one of the cleanest campaigns anyone had seen in a long time. The mudslingers stayed out of it and even the Super PACs were mostly silent. Mallory Hill was elected by the widest margin in modern history, and became the first woman to be elected President. Senator Rampling was gracious in defeat and vowed to help the new President in any way he could.

President Mallory Hill quoted August's report three times during her inauguration speech and made it clear that the United States was now ready to negotiate with anyone who was ready to have a peaceful and meaningful dialogue.

She acknowledged that we had made mistakes in the past and said that we would no longer pick and choose which countries we turned a blind eye to when it came to human rights. To everyone's surprise her words made a difference and groups that had previously been hostile to the United States reached out for dialogue instead of bullets. Mallory kept her promise to August and she kept her word to Jason as well.

Jason Rells became the Washington D.C. correspondent for the *Post*. Larry Molson never understood how the hell Jason had managed to transform himself overnight from pariah to the most favored journalist in D.C.

Larry got over it pretty fast, since Jason had been made into a hero by accompanying August Priest to the Middle East, and was ten times more popular than he had been. He still wrote an occasional "Rells Tells" column but they were now about issues that affected people and not about who was doing what to whom.

Those days were over for Jason. He thought about August often and he saw parts of him in Emily. He had begun to have feelings for her that were more than friendship. Emily wasn't only the most intelligent women he had ever known, she was also strikingly beautiful. Jason remembered the first time he had seen her when she wasn't wearing scrubs—with her hair done and makeup on—and he found himself unable to speak for a moment. That had never happened to him before.

He wondered what August would think if he knew he was starting to fall in love with his daughter. Those thoughts sometimes didn't end well for Jason.

Jason had also changed other things in his life: he limited himself to only one glass of scotch per week, he started to eat better, and he began to exercise. It was Emily who orchestrated the change in his behavior. She was, after all, a heart surgeon, and she made sure to point out how his bad habits would affect his health. She turned Jason on to jogging and sometimes on weekends they would run together. Jason liked to jog in the morning during the week and when he finished his run he would always made a smoothie in the blender Emily bought for him.

On this particular morning, Jason came in from his run and walked into the kitchen and went to the blender. The lid was on the counter and inside the blender was a hunting knife with an ivory handle bearing the initials AP. Jason should have been surprised, but he just smiled. August was always a few steps ahead of everyone else. Jason decided he and Emily would take a ride to West Virginia that weekend. He had something he needed to return.

The day the hostages were freed, Jason Rells had no way of knowing that his adventures with August Priest were only just beginning. Meeting August Priest would forever alter the rest of his life.

August and Jason will be back in *Unnatural Selection*, coming in early 2016.